Sunset Weddings

ANJ Press

Pittsburgh

SUNSET WEDDINGS
ANJ Press, First edition. March 2023.
Copyright © 2023 Amelia Addler.
Written by Amelia Addler.

Cover design by CrocoDesigns
Maps by MistyBeee

for the thrill of chance

Recap and Introduction to *Sunset Weddings*

Life gets even more exciting in the fourth installment of the Orcas Island series!

The series began when Claire caught a windfall inheritance and bought The Grand Madrona Hotel on Orcas Island. It was perhaps the best luck of her life – a life that had not been free of tragedy. Thirty years prior, her sister Holly, her brother-in-law, and her parents had died in a plane crash. Claire adopted Holly's daughters – Lucy, Lillian, and Rose – and they built a life together.

After her move to Orcas, Claire discovered her twin sister Becca, whom she believed to have perished in the plane crash, was still alive. Even better, they discovered Becca had a son, Marty, and he also moved to the island.

To top it all off, Chip, the manager at the hotel, proposed to Claire, and now she is in a whirlwind to plan the joyous event.

In the meantime, Lillian broke up with her boyfriend, Mason, and moved to the island to start over. She's quite happy with her new beginning until another ex-boyfriend, her high school sweetheart, pops back into her life...

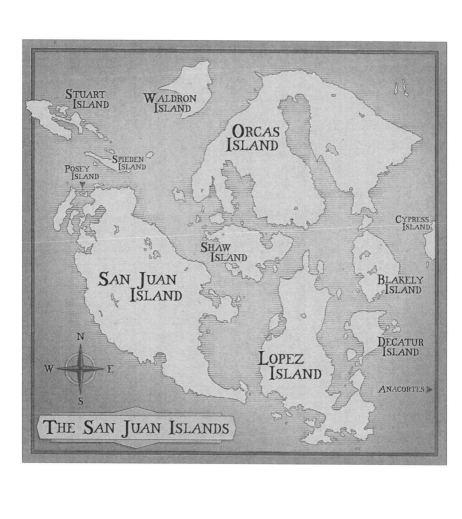

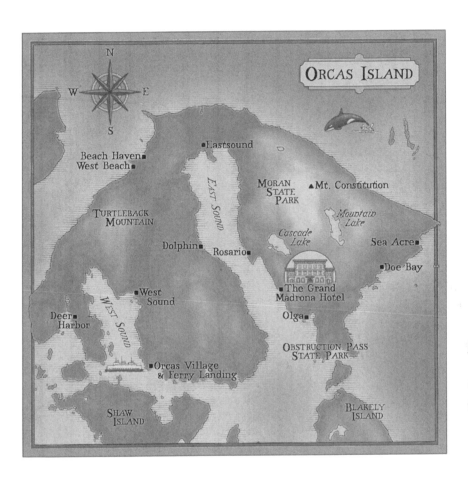

ORCAS ISLAND

N
W E
S

Eastsound

Beach Haven
West Beach

MORAN
STATE
PARK

▲ Mt. Constitution

EAST SOUND

TURTLEBACK
MOUNTAIN

Mountain
Lake

Cascade
Lake

Sea Acre

Dolphin

Rosario

Doe Bay

West
Sound

The Grand
Madrona Hotel

WEST SOUND

Deer
Harbor

Olga

OBSTRUCTION PASS
STATE PARK

Orcas Village
& Ferry Landing

SHAW
ISLAND

BLAKELY
ISLAND

Chapter One

Whenever Lucy started a sentence with, "Promise you won't be mad," Lillian had to decide if she should, or even could, make such a vow.

A promise of unconditional, blanketed calm was quite an ask, and when Lucy made the request, it implied the need for forgiveness as well.

It wasn't as though Lillian had a temper. She strived to be reasoned and composed, especially with her sisters. Lucy knew this, which made her prompt all the more concerning, especially since it was the first thing out of her mouth early that Saturday morning.

"Lucy," Lillian said evenly, "I'm not going to make a promise I can't keep."

"No, listen, it's not that bad. We have to go, though. Right now."

"Right now?" Lillian sighed. "I was about to put my laundry in."

"Well stop the presses!" Lucy threw Lillian's coat into her arms. "I wouldn't want to mess with your laundry plans."

"Where are we going?"

"That's the thing. Before I tell you, you have to promise you won't get mad at me."

So insistent. Lillian rolled her eyes. It wasn't like she was going to tell Lucy no. She just wanted to know what kind of trouble they were getting into.

"Why are you convinced I'll be mad?"

"I'll tell you after you get in the car." Lucy unlocked the door and swung it open, looking over her shoulder.

The entryway of their small apartment had looked like something out of a magazine ever since Lucy had convinced the landlord to let her spruce things up. In one weekend, she'd repainted the walls a robin's egg blue, installed white wainscoting, and constructed a chic mudroom near the door, complete with golden hooks and charming wicker baskets.

It was Pinterest-worthy. Lucy also kept the place obsessively clean, sometimes tucking Lillian's things away as she tidied, never to be found again.

Lillian pulled on her coat and made her way to the front door. "You're turning this into a low-key hostage situation, do you realize that?"

"Nah, it's not like that," Lucy said, a smile spreading across her face. "You keep telling me you want to say 'yes' to more things, so why not say 'yes' to me?"

Lillian laughed. It was true that she was trying to be open to new opportunities. So far, her move to Orcas Island had offered plenty of new things – a new climate, magnificent views of the ocean, and that one Pilates class Lucy had tricked her into attending.

That seemed like plenty for now.

"Let's go!" Lucy urged.

"How can I say yes to something when I don't even know what it is?"

"Do we ever really know what anything is?" Lucy mused, pulling open the door and waving a hand for Lillian to walk through.

"I mean, yes. Like I knew I was going to have some clean laundry, but now –"

"I'll do your laundry later." With long strides, Lucy reached her car and unlocked the doors. "It's Claire. She needs our help."

"Oh. Why would I be mad about that?"

Lillian never said no to helping family. Their mom – whom Lucy had called by her first name since their adoption thirty years prior – had been overwhelmed recently, though she would never admit it. The small wedding she had planned for September had ballooned into an event with over three hundred guests, and the wedding-related events were piling up.

The problem stemmed from Claire's unwillingness to say no. She was a people pleaser – Lillian could relate – and her friend Margie had become something of a bossy, rogue relative, taking everything into her own hands. Margie first pestered Claire into inviting too many people, then successfully planned an engagement party, a bridal shower, and a bachelorette party before she knew what was happening.

Lillian got into the car and as soon as she shut her door, Lucy pulled onto the street. "You know she never asks for help."

"I know," Lillian said. "Is something wrong at the hotel?"

Lucy narrowed her eyes. "Not exactly. Not wrong, no."

"Then what is it?" By this point, Lillian had imagined scenarios that were likely far worse than what was actually happening – a fire, or all of the hotel staff walking out, or a belligerent guest barricading themselves in one of the rooms. "Just spit it out. You're killing me."

"All right, fine. Did you hear they were having trouble getting bookings for the summer?"

"I did."

"It was weird, because usually tourists start coming in for Memorial Day and it's pretty steady all season."

"Right."

Lucy took a deep breath. "They figured out last week that the system on the website had been broken and no one could book anything."

"Oh no, you're kidding! Did Marty look at it?"

Lucy waved a hand, eyes still fixed on the road ahead. "Yeah, Marty came in and fixed it in like five minutes. But the damage was done. Bookings were still way down."

"Hm."

What was Lucy getting them into? An image flashed in Lillian's mind of being dressed as a mascot for the hotel. Maybe she'd be an orca, all black and white with a big, oversized head. She could envision the sweat dripping down her face as she spun a "Book your room now!" sign around at the ferry landing.

"So anyway," Lucy continued, "I happened to find a large group who needed a block of rooms for ten weeks."

"That's good, right?"

She nodded, shooting a hurried look at Lillian. "Yeah, there's just one little, tiny thing that makes it a bit complicated."

"Lucy! You make it so much worse when you do this. Just tell me already."

"Okay, fine. The group is shooting a show on the island, and the producer said he would only book with us if he got his own personal concierge – a liaison, he called it – to help him with things. I might've volunteered you."

Lillian looked out the window to avoid betraying any negative emotion on her face, but it wasn't nearly as bad as what she had imagined. It might be inconvenient to have to be a "liaison," but she worked from home, and she could make her own hours.

No, it wasn't bad at all. She was happy to help their mom however she could. Though her mom was doing much better recently with running The Grand Madrona Hotel, everyone needed help once in a while. It might be kind of fun, too, if she could see how a TV show was made.

"Are you mad?" Lucy asked, her face creased with lines.

Lillian shook her head. "No. I mean, it was kind of rude, and you should've asked me, but it's fine. I don't mind."

Lucy sighed and flipped her turn signal for the driveway leading to the hotel.

Spring was just beginning, and little green buds dotted the branches arching over the road. Birds flitted to and fro, beaks full of grass and branches for their nests, and the warm blue sky betrayed no hint of how biting the wind was.

Moving to Orcas Island was already changing Lillian. She went for runs in the morning, just as the sun appeared over the horizon, and always made a point to stop and admire the sweeping views of the ocean. It took her breath away every single time. In those quiet moments, she believed anything was possible.

Lucy was right; she needed to say yes and figure out the details later. Otherwise, how else would she find things she never would've agreed to do before?

They kept driving until The Grand Madrona Hotel came into view. Two gorgeous Madrona trees stood in front, their red bark standing out against the sand-colored stone walls. The trees' glossy green leaves, steadfast throughout the winter, swayed as the wind blew, unbothered by the gusts.

Lillian loved the hotel. She loved the art deco design, the grand entry, the intricate tile work, and the shining metal details. It was so romantic. She liked to imagine what it was like when it was first built in the 1920s. Was it all flapper dresses and long cigarettes and secret love affairs?

That was at least what Lillian wanted to believe.

"Oh shoot. I think that's his car," Lucy said, pulling into a parking spot. "I guess this starts now."

"Okay," Lillian said. "It seems kind of exciting. I'm surprised you didn't volunteer for it yourself."

Lucy unbuckled her seat belt and opened her door. "One last thing."

"What?"

With her back turned, Lucy added, "Your ex-boyfriend is the star of the TV show."

It took Lillian a moment to process what she'd heard. "Wait, what?"

Before she could get an answer, Lucy darted out of the car and into the morning sun.

Chapter Two

From the moment Dustin had suggested the San Juan Islands for the show, he knew there was a possibility of running into Lillian. He didn't believe it would happen, because he'd gone nearly ten years without seeing her, but he understood the risk.

He told himself that even whispering "San Juan" was a moment of madness, a flirtation with fate. He blamed his giddiness on the excitement of signing on for the show. How was he supposed to know that out of the half dozen ideas he had pitched to the executive producer, Gunther, the guy would fall in love with these islands?

At first, Dustin thought he could avoid an awkward reunion with Lillian if he stuck to San Juan Island. That lasted until Gunther made the decision to have the entire crew stay on Orcas Island, the same fifty-seven square mile island where Lillian had just moved.

Now all Dustin could do was regret.

Lillian was going to think he was a weirdo – a stalker! It wasn't like he kept tabs on her *all* the time. She was his first love, so of course he occasionally checked in to see what she was up to.

It wasn't weird or anything, but yes, he happened to know she'd moved to Orcas Island. She'd posted a picture of the ferry terminal with the caption "Excited for this new chapter!"

The water was clear, the skies were blue. It was pretty, that was all, and he got curious about the place. He went down a rabbit hole and got caught up in the wildlife on the San Juan Islands. How was he supposed to know that Gunther would actually take his half-hearted suggestion about filming the show there? It was like the guy had no ideas of his own.

No, that wasn't true. Gunther had lots of ideas. Dustin wasn't going to start thinking negatively about him now. Not after leaving his beloved veterinary practice in Oregon to take a chance on making a show with the guy. Gunther was eccentric, but he wasn't a bad person.

A voice carried through the parking lot and Dustin froze. He'd have known that voice anywhere.

Lucy.

"It's fabulous to finally meet you!" she yelled.

Across the parking lot, he could see her opening her arms and pulling Gunther into an embrace.

Would she spot him in his car? Dustin's chest tightened and he leaned forward, resting his chin on the steering wheel. Where was Lillian? Maybe she wasn't here. Maybe she'd moved back to Texas with that boyfriend.

Mason.

Dustin shouldn't have even known about the boyfriend. He told himself to not make it weird. *Play it cool. Try to –*

A car door slammed shut and Dustin turned, his stomach dropping in an instant.

Lillian. She was here after all.

He shrunk down, slamming his knees into the dashboard. He didn't care. He couldn't be seen.

Lillian walked by, not once casting her gaze in his direction. She looked different – her light brown hair was cut above her shoulders and her face was framed by some delicate bangs, blowing in the wind. Lillian brushed them aside, a small smile forming on her face as Lucy called her.

She hadn't changed much. She had the same delicate, fair skin, freckled near her nose. Those sharp cheekbones, her big blue eyes.

Dustin forced himself to take a breath. His chest still felt constricted. Was he having a panic attack? An asthma attack?

He didn't have asthma. Maybe it was all this sea air.

Surely Lillian must know he was here. Lucy must've told her.

He sat up a bit. They couldn't see him now. Lillian probably didn't even care that he was here. She wasn't the one who'd had her heart crushed all those years ago. She was the one who'd gotten to say no. She was the one who got to move on.

Not that Dustin hadn't moved on. He had. He wasn't the same boy she'd known then. That hopeless romantic, that sad little puppy she'd left behind, was long gone. He had nothing to prove to her.

The mad thought of running off crashed through his mind. He could forget about doing the TV show. Forget

Gunther. Forget that he'd have to grovel to get his job back at the vet clinic. He could start his car, drive to the ferry, and never come back.

His mind was whirring with the possibility when his cell phone rang.

Gunther.

"Where are you?" he asked. "We're getting ready to go into the hotel."

"I just got here," Dustin stammered. "I'll be there in a second."

He tucked his phone back into his pocket. He wasn't going to run away. Lillian would know, and she'd think he was being a coward.

No. He could face her. He could be mature.

She was being mature. In fact, she looked as serene as ever. Surely her heart wasn't thundering in her chest and sweat wasn't gathering at her brow. Like a normal person, she could see her high school boyfriend and say hello. She could be pleasant.

He could do it too. He could say hi, hello, how are you? Nice to see you again. How have you been? Oh yes, good, me too.

You know, he thought, *like a sane person.*

It was going to be fine. Once he saw her, the nerves would go away. That was all.

"Don't make it weird," he muttered to himself as he got out of the car.

Chapter Three

Before she regained her senses, Lillian spent a moment wondering how her newly ex-boyfriend Mason had gotten himself on a TV show.

She'd admit he was a good-looking guy, but he was addicted to work and lacked any TV-worthy interests. The only hobby he had was golfing, and that was usually work-related, too.

How had he landed himself a golfing show? Or had he signed up for The Bachelorette – or worse, The Bachelor – to make her jealous?

It wouldn't work, of course, and it seemed like far too much effort for him. He'd barely contacted her since she'd ended their relationship a few weeks ago, sending only a handful of civil texts about logistics, never once offering to talk things out.

Not that Lillian wanted to get back together with him, but after a seven-year relationship, she thought he'd at least make an effort to win her back.

He was too proud. Or maybe he didn't care. Maybe he'd never loved her at all.

Lillian didn't want it to bother her, and she knew it was silly, but she couldn't help it. It hurt.

It wasn't until she was numbly smiling and shaking hands with Gunther that she realized who Lucy had been talking about.

It wasn't Mason. It was her *other* ex-boyfriend, the one Lucy had casually mentioned weeks ago, only to never bring up again.

He was the only other boyfriend Lillian had ever had, her sweet, down-to-earth, heart-on-his-sleeve first love who, in contrast to Mason, had made no secret of how much she'd shattered his heart when she'd turned down his proposal: Doctor of Veterinary medicine and YouTube star Dustin McGuire.

The realization floated into her mind like an errant cloud on this clear day, and Lillian maintained her stiff smile, turning to Lucy, then back to Gunther, laughing and nodding like she was accepting an award.

"I loved that the hotel offered a concierge service, and I knew we couldn't stay anywhere else," Gunther said.

"Yes, of course. I am so happy to be of service," she heard herself reply.

Lucy beamed, nodding eagerly and playing her part, though the sideways glances she kept shooting betrayed how terrified she was of Lillian getting angry with her.

Coward. If Lucy had told her the truth, that their mom needed help with hosting Dustin's new boss and crew, she wouldn't have told her no. But it would have been nice to have a warning before her ex-boyfriend swooped back into her life!

"There's our star," Gunther said, waving a hand at someone behind them.

Lillian resisted turning around, instead fixing her eyes on Gunther and seeing him for the first time. His brown hair flowed past his shoulders, blond highlights delicately woven throughout. The bare skin of his chest was exposed through the V in his white shirt, and a single gold chain hung from his neck. His wrists were stacked with leather bracelets, and an expensive-smelling scent floated pleasantly with his every movement. He looked undeniably Hollywood, in a glamorous, bohemian sort of way.

"I made it," said a woman in a sing-song tone.

Lillian sighed. *Not Dustin.*

Gunther leaned forward and planted an exaggerated air kiss near the woman's cheek.

Lucy and Lillian had to avoid eye contact so they wouldn't laugh at the scene in front of them.

"Ladies, this is my producer, Ariel. She makes everything possible."

Lillian smiled and offered a handshake, which Ariel met with a dainty touch. She looked more like an actress than someone behind the scenes – her long, dark hair shone in the sun, and her copper-toned skin was smooth and blemish-free. She wore an oversized sweater that hung from her slim shoulders and looked effortlessly chic.

Lillian was also wearing an oversized sweater, though hers was more suited for an ugly sweater party. It was thick and too long in the sleeves, a red-nosed reindeer smiling on the front.

Even more mortifyingly, the back showed a reindeer butt with a fluffy cotton tail.

Her twin sister Rose had gotten it for her as a joke. Lillian thought it was funny then. Now she wished she'd burned it.

Why hadn't Lucy warned her Dustin would be here! She could've worn something – *anything* – else!

Her promise not to get angry was getting harder to keep. At least she had a jacket, and no one could see the reindeer butt. She would not take the jacket off for any reason.

"I thought you were the producer, Gunther?" Lucy asked.

Gunther brought his hands together, interlocking his fingers, and nodded. "I'm the executive producer. And the director, and one of the main writers." He waved a hand. "It's too much, I know. That's why I have Ariel. You two will be –"

Ariel cut him off, shouting and waving her hands in the air. "Dustin!"

There it was. The reunion Lucy had concocted, then concealed.

Lillian let out a breath before looking over her shoulder. Dustin walked toward them, pulling a wheeled bag and pushing a pair of black sunglasses to the top of his head.

It was like he'd stepped out of a dream. His hair was shorter and more stylish, no longer overflowing with curls, but the color was the same. Unlike Gunther, his sandy-colored hair was natural. His clothes were more fitted and sleek, but it was still him. Her Dustin, all dimples and charm.

He smiled, and before she realized it, Lillian was grinning back.

He put an arm up, yelling "Hey."

His voice hadn't changed at all, and hearing it in person was an altogether different experience than hearing it in one of his YouTube videos. It felt like the vibration hit her straight in the chest, sending flutters through her body.

Squeals erupted behind them, and Lucy and Lillian were quickly pushed out of the way as a group of women encircled Dustin. Some of them threw their arms around him in dramatic hugs, while others danced around with air kisses.

Lillian couldn't see his face, but she could hear his voice and his hearty, rolling laugh. Of course women lit up at the sight of him. She had always thought he was handsome, but now it was even more undeniable. He'd filled out from his gangly, high school self, all broad shouldered and muscular.

Who were these women? Fans? Models? They towered over her, with long legs and perfectly styled manes of cascading hair, all varying shades of blonde.

Lillian looked down at herself and tugged at the sleeve of her ugly sweater. Sweat was pooling in the creases of her hands. This was *not* the look she would've gone with if she'd had a choice.

Gunther air kissed everyone, then shooed the women away, pausing to point at Lillian.

"The hotel appointed a liaison for us. Dustin, this is Lilith."

She forced a smile. "Lillian."

Gunther clapped a hand to his chest. "So sorry, forgive me, I'm meeting so many new people this week. Lillian."

"It's no problem."

Dustin finally looked at her, still smiling a crooked smile. "We know each other, actually. Nice to see you both again."

"What!" Gunther clapped his hands together. "That's kismet, you know. Old friends? It's a good sign for our production."

"More than friends. They used to date," Lucy added, a smirk on her face.

"Why am I not surprised?" Gunther patted Dustin roughly on the back. "This guy gets all the most beautiful ladies."

Ha. *Smooth, Gunther.*

Still, Lillian felt like she'd been trampled by the stampede of models and rushed to defend her own honor. "It was a long time ago."

Dustin nodded. "It was. Back when I still believed in love."

Gunther busted out a hearty laugh, and Lillian forced a smile, her heart shrinking beneath her reindeer sweater.

"I'll grab your number, Lillian," Gunther said, pulling out his cell phone. "I think we'll start scouting tomorrow. We want to have everything nailed down before the rest of the crew arrives."

"Sure, it's – "

Lucy cut her off. "You can get it from Dustin."

They all turned to look at him. Dustin was staring at his phone. He looked up and scratched his eyebrow with his thumb. "Actually, I'll need it too."

Her already shrunken heart dropped into her stomach. *He'd deleted her number.*

Lillian darted a hand to her torso, then realized what she was doing and instead reached for Gunther's phone. He handed it over without looking at her, talking to Dustin about his flight, as she silently typed her number into his phone.

"There. Call any time," she said, forcing a smile. "Everyone at The Grand Madrona is so excited to have you."

Gunther grasped her shoulder. "Thanks Lillian. I'll be in touch. Dustin, let's go. We've both got suites, but don't tell the rest of the crew." He laughed, already turning to leave.

They walked through the front doors of the hotel and disappeared from her view. Lillian stood, staring.

"Now remember," Lucy said, slowly shrinking away. "You promised not to get mad."

She turned around and started the trek back to the car. "I need to get my laundry going. Are you coming?"

Chapter Four

They returned to the car in silence. It was a rare event where Lucy didn't know what to say. Lillian was clearly mad at her, but she hadn't envisioned it going that way!

In Lucy's mind, Lillian would've been a bit surprised to see Dustin, but once he hugged her and said how nice it was to see her, she'd be all smiles.

That was the first problem. Dustin hadn't hugged her. He didn't have the chance! He was rushed around by Gunther and promptly overrun by a pack of blonde clones.

What were those women doing anyway? They couldn't be part of the crew. There was no way.

Why did they all look alike? They even dressed alike. They must be Gunther's type...or maybe Dustin's.

No.

Not Dustin's type. Lillian was his type. Lucy was sure of it.

Lucy got in the car, fussed with her seat belt, and started the engine. Lillian followed a moment later, buckling in and staring silently ahead.

"It's killing me," Lucy finally said. "Just get it out of the way. Please yell at me."

"I'm not going to yell at you," Lillian said simply, looking at her hands and twisting a gold ring on her finger.

Lucy turned to her. "Come on, I know you're mad. I deserve whatever you have to say." She let out a sigh. " I knew if I'd told you Dustin would be here, you wouldn't have come."

Lillian finally looked at her. "That's not true. I'd still want to help, but if I'd have known Dustin was going to be here, I could've at least changed out of this sweater!"

Lucy's gaze drifted until she locked eyes with the goofy-looking reindeer on Lillian's chest. She darted a hand over her mouth. "I don't know how I missed that."

"Oh, you don't know how you missed me being dressed like a five-year-old?" She crossed her arms over her chest and let out a breath. "Because I'm sure everyone else saw."

"You could have zipped your jacket."

Lillian shut her eyes. "I wasn't thinking."

Lucy looked down. It wasn't funny. She shouldn't laugh. She *couldn't* laugh.

A laugh burst out of her anyway and she rushed to say, "I'm sorry! It's not funny."

"No, Lucy, it isn't!" Lillian laughed, too, but only briefly, before closing her eyes again and shaking her head. "If you had at least told me about Dustin, I could have mentally prepared for that moment."

Lucy winced. "I'm sorry. It wasn't that bad, was it?"

"I'm not sure what I expected, but Dustin seemed like he couldn't care less about seeing me. What's with my ex-boyfriends not caring about me? Am I that forgettable?"

"What? No!" They'd been sitting there long enough. Lucy didn't want Dustin to see them out there arguing about him.

She put the car into reverse and pulled out of the parking spot. "You're not forgettable. I don't buy Dustin's act for a second."

"He deleted my number from his phone, Lucy. He clearly never planned to speak to me again."

"No, he would only have deleted your number if he was worried he might try to contact you, which is what you do when you still care about someone."

Lillian rolled her eyes. "Yeah, probably like ten years ago, and then he completely forgot about me." She paused. "Which is fine. It's not like I expected him to still be in love with me or anything."

Lucy smiled to herself. She wasn't so sure about that. She hadn't told Lillian, but about six months ago, before Lillian had broken up with Mason, Lucy had gotten a notification on one of her Instagram pictures. It was an old one of her, Lillian, and Rose on a sister's trip.

The notification was from Dustin, of all people. He must have liked it by accident, and he undid it as soon as it happened, but the damage was done. Lucy knew he had been creeping on pictures of Lillian. *Old* pictures.

He still cared.

Lillian continued. "He seemed so...cold. I know he's a celebrity now, but –"

"He's not a celebrity," Lucy said with a snort. "He makes videos about potty training puppies on YouTube. It's cute, but come on."

"He has a *million* subscribers, Lucy! That's at least a million people who turn to him for veterinary advice."

"Like I said, it's cute, but whatever. I don't buy his cool persona for a second. The only reason he'd act so cold towards you is if he still had feelings for you."

"Don't start, Lucy." She wagged a finger at her. "You get these ideas and you think everyone is secretly in love and –"

"That's not what I think," Lucy said, but of course it was exactly what she thought. "You said it yourself. You were never happier than when you were with Dustin."

Lillian groaned. "Is that what this is about? All because, in a moment of weakness, I compared my recent breakup to my high school boyfriend? That was ages ago. We were kids! Of course life was easier then."

"It was more than that," Lucy argued. She'd never heard her sister say something that dramatic. How could she ignore a comment like that? How could she not try to reunite them? "You were young, but you were still you. Even in high school you were serious and mature, and Dustin was like a firework that livened everything up. You were perfect together."

"Yeah." Lillian's voice was quiet. "He's taken off, and I'm still dull, serious Lillian."

"You're not dull. You kept Dustin from burning the house down – literally, do you remember that? When he almost burned his parents' house down trying to make dinner for you?"

She shook her head. "We were baking a cake for his mom's birthday, and while we waited for it to cool he tried to make me broiled s'mores."

"Broiled s'mores!" Lucy cackled. "And the marshmallows caught on fire?"

"Yes, and the parchment paper they were on did, too."

"See? A perfect match." They laughed, and Lucy went on. "Not like Mason. He wasn't good for you. He was like a big, gray rock tied around your neck."

"He wasn't that bad," Lillian said. "We just wanted different things in life."

"Right." She reached a crossroads. They could either go back to their apartment or go into town for breakfast. After a moment of hesitation, she turned into town. She owed Lillian breakfast. "Mason wanted to be boring and sit on his pile of money, while you wanted to feel happiness again."

Lillian laughed. "Yeah, I wanted to break up with him so I could spend my time hanging around Dustin and looking pathetic."

"Dustin doesn't think you're pathetic! He still likes you."

Lillian laughed. "Stop. Seriously, you're making things up that aren't there. Where are we going?"

"I'm taking you to an apology breakfast," she said. "And I'm not making anything up. Why else would he act so strange?"

"Probably because you awkwardly announced that we'd dated!"

"I was trying to get a reaction out of him," Lucy said. "It worked."

"Yeah, the reaction was that he said he didn't believe in love anymore." Lillian groaned and hid her eyes behind her hands. "Do you think it's because of me?"

"Because you refused his hand in marriage when you were eighteen?" Lucy shrugged. "Hm, sounds like he's not over it, doesn't it?"

Lillian slumped in her seat. "I never wanted to hurt him."

"I still don't understand why you said no."

"Because we were eighteen! It was a terrible idea."

"You didn't have to break up with him, though," Lucy countered. "It didn't make any sense. Whenever I asked you about it, you'd get all quiet and weird."

"I had my reasons. It was the right thing to do."

Lucy pulled into an on-street parking spot. "That sounds silly."

"I never told you because I was embarrassed."

"What? You were too embarrassed to tell me, the queen of being embarrassing?"

Lillian flashed a smile, but kept staring at her hand and twisting that ring around her finger. "Dustin was always a dreamer. He got it into his head that we would both go to Ohio State. He wanted to go there for his undergrad degree, and then stay on for veterinary school."

"That's what he did, right? So he's not that much of a dreamer. He made it happen."

"Lucy, I didn't get into Ohio State. The only school I got into was a branch campus of the University of Washington."

Lucy frowned. She vaguely remembered the pile of letters rolling in for Lillian after she had applied to schools, but she didn't remember much else. "You never said anything about Ohio State."

"I didn't tell anyone. I wanted it to all go away. It's stupid, I know."

Lucy's mouth dropped open. "Did you ever tell Dustin?"

"No, because I knew he wouldn't have gone without me. I would've held him back, because I was too dumb to get in."

"You are not dumb, Lillian. Take it back."

"No." Lillian shrugged. "I'm not academically gifted."

"You weren't a good test taker, big deal. You got better. Now take it back!"

She waved a hand. "Fine. I take it back."

"You wouldn't have held him back. He would've found a different way to achieve his dreams."

She raised an eyebrow. "Do you really believe that?"

"Of course. Maybe if you finally tell him, he'll forgive you for breaking his heart and you can live happily ever after!"

"I think he's far beyond needing to forgive me," Lillian said. "He can comfort himself with the herds of beautiful women who squeal in excitement when he walks into a room, while I fetch coffee for Gunther."

Lucy grimaced. "You are mad at me."

"No, it's fine. Everything is fine. Do you want to get some breakfast?" Lillian opened the car door and stepped out onto the sidewalk.

Just like that, the topic was done. Lillian wouldn't bring it up again. Lucy didn't want to force it, but...

To her, it was obvious that Dustin still had feelings for Lillian. She hadn't been sure before, but after seeing him, it was clear as day.

Further, Lillian couldn't expect to say something as dramatic as "I've never been happier than when I was with Dustin" and expect Lucy to do nothing!

They just needed a little help, which Lucy was happy to provide.

She got out of the car. This was going to be interesting.

Chapter Five

After years of imagining what it would be like to see Lillian again, Dustin was disappointed.

Not in Lillian – she was the picture of grace. She hadn't missed a beat when Gunther had called her by the wrong name, or when the crew descended on the hotel like a flock of wild geese. And though Dustin was mortified, she had made no mention of how peculiar it was for him to show up, out of the blue, and stay at her mom's hotel.

Lillian was polite and welcoming. To top it all off, she was as beautiful as the day they'd parted. In the brief moment where he dared to look at her, it felt like he'd traveled through time. He was eighteen again, pleading for her to reconsider, to take him back and forget his foolish proposal.

What a dunce he was, then and now. It didn't matter if it was twelve years ago or the present. He was still a dunce.

He thought he could handle seeing her again and at least pretend to be unaffected, like a normal person. He wanted to be cool, but he had been so cool that he completely froze. He'd hardly said anything to her, and when he did speak, he admitted to deleting her number like a bitter ex.

Who does that?

He wasn't bitter. He'd deleted her number years ago in a desperate attempt to keep himself from reaching out to her. It was pathetic, and he wished it hadn't come out like it did. He wasn't able to think at the time, though, and he despised himself for it.

Dustin ruminated for the rest of the night, all through the dinner Gunther forced them to attend in the hotel's restaurant, and long after he'd laid down in the dark to try to get some sleep.

Staring up at the ceiling, all he could see was her face. Memories flooded back, crashing in like waves, the pain as fresh as though she'd just refused him.

It was impossible to sleep. Why was he like this? She'd clearly moved on and lived a healthy life. Dustin, on the other hand – had he ever recovered?

Maybe it wasn't her, exactly. Maybe it was the fact that Lillian was the first in a pattern of his relationships. Women wanted nothing to do with him. He didn't know why that was, but after watching his friends happily marry and start families, Dustin knew something was wrong with him. His ex-fiancée could speak to that.

After a few hours of fitful sleep, the sun began its rise and he finally gave up. The views from his room were incredible, with East Sound framed by mountains on the distant side of the island. He spent too long gazing out the window, and despite having plenty of time to get ready, Dustin fell behind schedule. He was still rushing when a knock rang through his hotel room door.

Ariel's voice carried through. "Are you ready to go?"

"Just a second!" He threw on a shirt and pulled the door open. At least one of them was on top of things. "Hey. How's it going?"

"Not bad. A little tired. Gunther kept me up until three because he wanted to brainstorm ideas." She rubbed her face and let out a little laugh.

"Yeesh. I thought it was bad that he forced the restaurant staff to stay an hour late so we could finish our team building dinner."

Gunther was big on team building. He talked Dustin's ear off about the importance of culture, stressing that the experience of shooting the show was just as important as the final product.

It was interesting how Gunther approached life – he was a big-picture sort of guy, all warmth and hope. It was good. He wanted people to have fun, to have an experience.

Dustin was certainly having an experience.

They called the elevator and chatted on the ride down, though Dustin had a hard time focusing on their conversation.

How had Claire been able to buy this hotel? Both Lillian and Dustin had never had much money growing up, and this place was no dumpy shack. The hotel was gorgeous. Had Claire won the lottery or something?

So many questions he didn't dare ask. The elevator doors opened to the lobby, the shining marble floors bustling with life. Gunther was front and center, standing beneath a grand chandelier and having a loud argument on the phone.

"I didn't say you were needed yet, so if you're on the island, that's on you. We're not going to start shooting until we have everything nailed down." A pause. "I don't know. A few weeks? We're doing this the right way."

Dustin shot a look at Ariel. "Is everything okay?"

"I'm sure it is," she said in a low voice. "There was some confusion with one of the cameramen."

"Is it unusual to spend so much time on location before starting to film?"

Ariel squinted, biting her lip. "I'm not really sure. I've mostly worked as a production assistant until now, so I'm not normally involved this early." She rushed another laugh. "Of course I'm ready to do everything we need to do to make this show succeed."

"Of course," Dustin replied. It wasn't that he didn't have faith in her. He had no idea how things were supposed to work. He was just trying to keep himself from looking like a fool, which was difficult to do with his habit of speaking before thinking.

He kept his eyes on the front door of the hotel, trying to mentally prepare himself to see Lillian again. This time, he wasn't going to be weird. He was going to act like a normal person, as though a breakup from over a decade ago didn't still haunt him.

Should he try to say something nice? He wanted to tell her she looked great, but he was afraid it might betray too much about how he felt.

She did look great, though. Lillian had to know that already. She didn't need him to tell her. It was probably best to keep the comments to himself.

He was still staring at the door when he heard Gunther end his call and say, "Good thing you're here. I was hoping to talk to you."

"At your service," Lillian's voice answered.

Where had she come from? Dustin spun around, unable to keep the stunned look off his face. "Lillian!"

She smiled. "Morning, Dustin. It's nice to see you again."

"It's nice to see you too." He paused. That didn't seem like enough, so he decided to make it more awkward. "And it's nice to see a familiar face."

She nodded, and Gunther started talking again. "I was hoping you could get me a list of the scientists in the area."

Lillian stared at him. "The scientists?"

Gunther nodded. "Dustin mentioned there's a lab here that does research on mollusks or something?"

"Oh," Lillian clasped her hands together. "The Friday Harbor Laboratories, yeah. They do all kinds of marine research. I actually have a contact there; I'd be happy to put you in touch."

He put both hands on her shoulders. "Lillian, you're an angel."

She laughed. "If you say so. Is there anything else you need today?"

"We'll start there," he said, pulling his hands away and clapping decisively. "Ariel, I need to talk to you about the camera situation."

They stepped aside, leaving Dustin and Lillian to stare at each other.

Dustin spoke first. "This hotel is stunning."

"Thank you. Mom loves it."

He nodded, feeling the freeze coming over him. He couldn't let it happen again. "You look fantastic, by the way. Sorry we couldn't talk more yesterday. It was so crazy and –"

"Oh, don't be sorry. You're a big star." She smiled, seemingly genuinely, her beautiful blue eyes lighting up. "I don't expect you to remember the little people."

A laugh burst out of him. The freeze was rapidly thawing. It was silly to think he couldn't face her – there was nothing between them anymore. She wasn't holding a grudge. He could laugh with her like an old friend.

Yes, that's all she was. An old friend, and he could show her he wasn't the same loser she'd turned down all those years ago. He wasn't in danger of falling in love with her again. Love was a sham. He'd at least learned that in the years since they'd parted. "I'm not a star. To be honest, I don't know how I got here. I mean, on this show."

"I'm sure that you..." Her voice trailed off, and her eyes drifted behind him.

"Is everything okay?" he asked, turning around and spotting what had caused her smile to fade.

It was her boyfriend – or her ex-boyfriend? Mason.

Dustin was familiar with him from Lillian's Instagram, though he had to be sure to not betray that fact.

"I finally made it," Mason yelled from across the lobby, hands outstretched. "You're right, this island is amazing."

Without realizing it, Dustin's right hand formed into a fist at his side.

Mason walked over, stepping in front of Dustin as though he didn't exist. "Why do you look so surprised?"

"I had no idea you were coming," Lillian stammered. "I haven't heard from you in weeks."

"Don't I get a hug?"

Lillian stood, stiff, as Mason put his arms around her. After a moment, she patted him lightly on the back and pulled away. "What are you doing here?"

"Maybe we should find somewhere quiet to talk?" Mason asked.

Dustin was sick of looking at the back of this guy's head. "Hey there," he said, tapping him on the shoulder. "I'm Dustin. Nice to meet you."

Mason looked over her shoulder and nodded. "What's up?"

"I'm busy today, Mason," Lillian said slowly. "If you want to talk –"

He cut her off. "We need to talk. The past few weeks have been torture."

She raised her eyebrows. "Oh? It seemed like –"

"I was giving you time to cool off, but now I realize I need to step it up."

"Step it up?" she repeated.

"Come on. You didn't think I'd let you just walk out of my life, did you?"

So he was the *ex*-boyfriend.

Lillian scowled at him and Dustin relaxed his fist. Apparently, not every ex got a warm welcome from her.

It didn't seem like such a bad day after all.

Chapter Six

What on earth was going on? Was this her punishment for feeling sorry for herself when Mason didn't make an effort to win her back?

Lillian stared at Mason, her thoughts slow, as though they were trudging through a bog.

This was bad. She didn't want this. She wanted him to go back to ignoring her. She didn't want him to say things like he wouldn't "let" her walk out of his life.

"We need to find a time to talk." Mason pulled out his phone and opened his schedule. "I'm free for the rest of the afternoon. What works for you?"

Oh, how she hadn't missed living by that calendar of his. "I'm busy, actually."

He nodded. "It's okay. I don't leave until tomorrow afternoon. We can meet up in the morning."

"I can't. I'm going wedding dress shopping, and I don't know if –"

"Not for yourself, I hope," he said, cutting her off. "Unless you've changed your mind and want to run away with me?"

"No," she said quickly, "it's for my mom. We're all going to the mainland to shop. We're catching an early ferry out."

He let out a sigh and put his phone back in his pocket. "You always wanted me to be more spontaneous, Lil, but it makes it hard to make plans."

She blinked at him, and he cracked a smile.

"I'm just kidding, I know this is my fault. I should've told you I was coming, but I wanted to surprise you."

"Mission accomplished," Dustin said, taking a step back.

Mason looked over his shoulder and laughed. "Yeah man, tell me about it."

Lillian stood, staring at the two of them. It was like something out of a fever dream. Mason was smiling broadly, but the smile didn't reach his eyes. She knew him too well. It was a strained look. Desperate.

Was it because he recognized Dustin? That seemed unlikely. Mason had never expressed any interest in Lillian's former romantic life, and she hadn't had any social media in high school.

Dustin was smiling, too, but with only the slightest curve of his mouth, as though trying to hold himself back.

Was this funny to him? Mason made it sound like she'd refused another proposal. Dustin probably thought she'd made a habit of it.

It wasn't true, though, and as bad as she felt for Mason in that moment, she also felt the urge to explain they hadn't been engaged and she wasn't some serial heartbreaker. Mason had never technically proposed. He kept saying he would, and then he'd hold it over her head until it became a sort of vague threat.

Everything she wanted him to change was for "after we're engaged," as if it was some idyllic future life for her to chase.

They were both still looking at her. She had to say something. Lillian cleared her throat. "I'm doing some work on behalf of the hotel."

"I understand," Mason said, nodding. "It's okay. You know what? I'm going to be here a lot."

"Oh?"

He pressed his hands together, fidgeting with his fingers. "I am. I'm trying, Lil. I miss you. I can't stop thinking about you. I've been –" Mason paused, looking past her. He stuck an arm in the air. "Gunther? I didn't know you were staying here."

Gunther walked toward them at a brisk pace, Ariel trailing a few steps behind. He waved back to Mason before turning to mumble something to Ariel.

This was her chance. Dustin and Mason were distracted, and Lillian could excuse herself if she moved quickly enough. She opened her mouth to announce she was leaving, but it was too late. Ariel had already taken off toward the front doors.

"It's the best hotel on the island," Gunther said, smiling warmly at Lillian.

"It really is," Dustin added, still with a bemused look on his face.

"Thank you." Lillian kept smiling, her face and shoulders stiff.

"Of course." Gunther pointed a finger at Mason. "I hope you're not trying to steal my liaison."

Mason put his hands up. "I wouldn't dream of it. Lillian and I – well, we have a history."

He looked at her hopefully, and she felt her insides curling.

What a fool she was to think he was handling the breakup so well. He was just recovering from the shock, and now he was back on his feet, ready to annoy her.

Gunther's eyes settled on her, and she again struggled with finding something to say. Understanding flickered across his expression and she fully expected him to make a comment about her dating all the eligible bachelors or something, but mercifully, he was kinder than that.

He clapped his hands together and said, "Lillian, I'll try not to monopolize too much of your time. Dustin and I are going to see a few spots on the island today. We'll be in touch later?"

"Sounds great," she said. "I'll reach out to my friend at the lab and get back to you right away."

He shook her hand. "Thanks again. Talk to you soon."

Dustin nodded at them both, then walked off with Gunther.

Lillian watched them for a moment before turning back to Mason. Before she could say anything, he started talking.

"Don't give me that look! You have to give me a chance to win you back, Lil. There's no reason we shouldn't be together."

"No reason?" To think, a few seconds ago she was worried about hurting his feelings. "You really think there's *no reason* we shouldn't be together?"

"I know you're mad at me, but you didn't even give us a chance to work it out. Seven years together, and it's all down the drain? For what? Because I'm a few weeks late coming to visit here? Come on."

"That's not why we broke up, Mason." How was he always able to twist things to make her sound ridiculous? She closed her eyes and took a deep breath. "We want different things in life. Please don't do this."

"I have to do what my heart tells me," he said, drawing himself up.

"We tried, Mason, we did," she said. "But you're focused on work, and I wanted more from our life, and –"

"I'm not going to focus on work anymore," he said quickly. "I'm going to focus on you. That's why I'm here."

Lillian shook her head. She wasn't having this conversation with him, especially because he could talk circles around her. It seemed the one thing he couldn't do was listen. "I have to go."

"How about dinner tonight?"

"No, I can't." She paused. "I mean, we can't."

"I'll talk to Gunther and get you off the hook."

"I don't want to be off the hook. I'm doing this to help my mom." Her voice rose a bit too much. She told herself to calm down. "How do you even know Gunther?"

He shrugged, the confidence rebuilding in his face. "We have a mutual friend on the island."

"What's that supposed to mean?"

"I'll tell you at dinner."

She let out a sigh. "Goodbye, Mason."

"Wait, no. Don't leave." He grabbed onto her wrist. "And don't get all mad at me. I'm just trying to have an air of mystery to remind you why you love me."

She pulled her arm away. "Mason."

"Fine. His name is Aaron Forest. He's the CEO of Stardust Oil. He has a property on the island, and my company might be doing business with him."

She crossed her arms. "Ah. So are you here to see me, or to do work?"

He leaned in and grabbed her by the hand. "Why can't it be both?"

She pulled her hand away. They had spent months of their relationship fighting about his endless work trips. It was like he couldn't help himself, and now he admits this visit was also a work trip?

He was infuriating. At least she didn't have to feel bad about not going to dinner with him. "Enjoy your work trip, Mason."

"I'm only working with him as an excuse to see you."

She turned to leave.

"You won't get rid of me that easily!" he added.

Lillian paused and took a deep breath. No need to make a scene. "Enjoy your stay!"

She walked away, disappearing into her mom and Chip's office as quickly as she could.

Once she was convinced Mason was gone, Lillian went back to her apartment to sort out the business with the lab. Lucy had gotten to know Kelly, one of the graduate students there, after saving Grindstone Farm. Lillian only knew her in passing, and she felt a bit awkward reaching out to her about Dustin's show, but she made the call anyway.

Kelly was thrilled to hear from her, and to have a chance to showcase the lab. Her research focused on the effect of ocean acidification on Dungeness Crabs, but she said if that was too niche for Dustin's show, she could talk about the mussel population, or walk them through tidal pools, or whatever they wanted. She said she was happy to take Gunther's call any time of day, and that she'd even come to Orcas Island to chat if he preferred.

That had been easy enough. She sent Kelly's information off to Gunther and sat on the couch.

Her first task as a liaison had gone well. Except for her ex-boyfriend showing up out of nowhere.

The more she thought about it, the less Lillian believed he had come up with the idea on his own. If anyone had been in on it, it was Lucy.

She waited until Lucy got back from her outing with Rob to confront her.

"How was horseback riding?" Lillian asked, planted on the couch with her arms crossed.

"It was so much fun. They put Rob on this really mean horse, Bucky. It was hilarious. He didn't listen to Rob at all. At one point, Bucky was off grazing on some grass and the instructor had to get off her horse to drag him back to the trail." Lucy giggled. "I loved it. They had me on this little pony. I thought I would be too heavy for her, but it was fine. She was sweet as can be."

"That's nice."

Lucy flopped onto the couch. "What's wrong? Are you mad at me?"

"Why would you think I'm mad at you?"

"Because you're sitting there with your arms crossed and you've got an angry look on your face," Lucy said matter-of-factly. "You're still mad about Dustin, aren't you? Listen, I'm sorry. In my head it was all going to go differently. It was supposed to be...I don't know, fun?"

"This isn't about Dustin. It's about Mason."

Lucy frowned. "Mason? What about him?"

"You're going to pretend like you don't know?"

Lucy put her hands up in apparent surrender. "I didn't do anything to Mason!" She paused and looked down. "I *thought* about sending him a nasty message a few months ago, but you broke up with him and I didn't have to."

"Why were you going to send him a nasty message?"

She waved a hand, then stood to cross the small span to the kitchen. "He was making you so sad. He kept calling and starting fights with you."

"So you don't want me to get back with him?" Lillian said slowly.

"Absolutely not!" Lucy said, taking a gulp of water. "Why? Are you thinking of getting back with him?"

Lillian laughed, the tension easing from her shoulders. "No, but he showed up at the hotel and declared that he was going to win me back. I assumed you had something to do with it."

"Ew! No!" Lucy's mouth hung open. "What did you do? What did you say?"

Lillian was satisfied Lucy had nothing to do with Mason's sudden appearance, and she went on to tell her the story from start to finish.

When she was done, Lucy stared at the floor. "Huh."

"What?"

"It's just strange. Makes me feel weird."

"Me too." Lillian hid her face in her hands. "Actually, this is kind of embarrassing. I was a little sad because he hadn't as much as texted me after we broke up, and I thought he never loved me."

"Aw, Lillian! Of course he loved you. Still does, apparently."

She dragged her hands down her face, pulling at her cheeks. "Now here he is, declaring his love in the public square. I could kick myself. I should've told him it was over, that we wouldn't be seeing each other again."

"You can still tell him that," Lucy said. "You can send a text."

"No, that's mean. I don't want to be mean to him. He looked genuinely sad, like he hadn't realized we were really broken up until now. Plus, Dustin was just standing there, and...ugh. It was just bad, Lucy. It was all bad."

"Fine. We can send a pigeon. Or I can deliver him a hand-written note to the hotel. I don't mind."

Lillian laughed. "Thanks, but you've done enough."

"Fair." Lucy shifted her weight. "What I don't get is this oil company CEO friend."

Lillian shrugged. "He's just doing business with them."

"Yeah, but that doesn't explain why Gunther knows him."

"Who? Mason?"

"No, why Gunther is also friends with the oil guy – Aaron Forest. Gunther's got this whole earthy, nature vibe going on, yet he's hanging out with an oil executive?"

"I guess rich guys hang out."

Lucy shook her head. "I don't buy it. Something doesn't smell right."

Lillian let out a sigh. "Why do you always look for conspiracies?"

"Because there are a lot of shady rich dudes." She leaned in. "Now, obviously I don't want you to get back with Mason, but *maybe* you could entertain his attention just a little bit longer to figure out what's going on between Gunther and Oil Aaron?"

"Lucy! I'm not going to string Mason along to feed one of your conspiracy hobbies."

She narrowed her eyes. "Don't you want to know why they're all friends? What if they're planning something nefarious for the island?"

"What if they're not?"

Lucy tapped a finger on her chin. "What if Dustin is involved?"

Lillian fell silent. She wouldn't deny that Dustin seemed different than before, but had he changed so much that he might do something "nefarious" on the island?

"You don't have to hang out with Mason," Lucy continued. "Maybe I'll pay him a visit, see how he's doing."

"Please don't. You'll only encourage him, and I think you've done enough to encourage my exes."

She bit her lip. "All right, I'll keep my nose out of it. But if you hear anything, you have to tell me!"

"Of course."

There wouldn't be anything to tell. Lucy had too vivid of an imagination. She was still riding the high of saving Grindstone Farm from being sold off, and from keeping the Grand Madrona Hotel out of a developer's hands. To be honest, if it weren't for her, the hedge fund would've had its way on Orcas Island.

Lillian wouldn't say it out loud, but Lucy could be on to something. "Let's talk about it tomorrow. Do you know where we're going for these dresses?"

"Oh yes!" Lucy leapt from the couch and grabbed a stack of papers. "I made an itinerary for the day. We've got four dress shops to hit, and I've gone to the website for each to pre-select some gowns I think Claire would like. Do you want to see?"

Anything to take her mind off Mason. And to help her forget that half smile on Dustin's face. "Yes please."

Lillian made a bowl of popcorn and they settled onto the couch to revel in the wedding excitement.

Chapter Seven

As silly as it was, Claire was excited for the shopping trip. It wasn't so much about the wedding dresses – in fact, any event where she became the center of attention was mortifying – but she was looking forward to the experience. Lucy and Lillian were coming, and Margie had volunteered to drive when they reached the mainland. Becca had even flown into Bellingham for the day, with a plan to come back to Orcas Island after and stay for a week.

It was going to be a blast. Claire's only regret was that Rose wasn't able to come. Her work was too demanding, and she lived far enough away that dropping in wasn't possible. She promised to make a video call when she had a chance, so that would be nice.

Chip drove them to the ferry terminal early that morning. Claire insisted he didn't need to, but he didn't want to be left out, and he was always looking for excuses to be sweet.

"Have fun, ladies," he said, one arm hanging out of the window of his truck. "And Lucy?"

"Yes, Not-So-Evil Stepfather?"

A scowl crossed his face, but he knew better than to engage with her. She'd only come up with a more annoying nickname.

"Try to convince Claire to spend some money on herself, will you?"

Lucy let out a dramatic sigh. "I'll see what I can do, but you know how she is."

Claire leaned in and gave him a kiss on the cheek. "A wedding dress is a silly thing to waste money on."

"I agree," Lillian said, slipping on a pair of sunglasses.

Lucy glared at them. "Both of you need to improve your attitudes. Goodbye, Not-So-Evil Stepfather!"

Chip shook his head, grinning. "Have fun."

They walked onto the ferry and were surprised to find Margie was already on board. She had apparently traveled from San Juan Island early that morning to meet them.

"You didn't have to do that," Claire said, giving her a hug.

"I wanted to. And, oh my goodness, you need to see the van. I borrowed it from my neighbor."

She led them downstairs to the car deck, weaving between the parked cars, motorcycles, and trucks until they arrived at a green minivan.

"It's a nice-looking minivan, Margie," Lucy said, studying it. "Good job, I guess?"

Margie smiled widely and walked to the back of the van, pulling a four-foot slip of pink fabric off the side.

"It's a car flag! I have them on both sides!"

A laugh escaped from Lillian as Claire leaned over to make out the white bubble letters on the fabric. It read **BRIDE'S RIDE!**

"Do you like it?" Margie asked, still beaming.

"It's very cute."

"I thought so," she said, nodding approvingly.

"It makes us look like we're riding in a Barbie construction vehicle," Lucy added.

"It does not," Margie said. "It's fun! And we will look fun riding in it."

"You're right. I'm just mad I didn't think of it," Lucy said before herding them all back up the stairs and into the galley.

After buying coffees, they stepped onto the windy deck. It was a beautiful, sunny morning, though there were a few crisp white clouds floating above them. They were passing between Blakeley and Decatur Island, and Claire stood at the railing admiring the rocky, sloping hills covered in lush green trees.

Lucy accosted a bystander to take their picture, and afterward, they settled onto a bench.

"Is Aunt Becca going to meet us at the first shop?" asked Lillian.

Lucy nodded. "She might even beat us there, which is good, because I can have her pull a few dresses so they're ready."

Margie clapped her hands together. "Do you have pictures?"

"Of course." She reached into her purse and pulled out a stack of papers. Margie scooted closer.

Claire stared at them, her mouth hanging open. "Was anyone going to show me these dresses before they were put on my body?"

Lucy waved a hand. "You're going to love them. I have impeccable taste."

Claire let out a sigh and smiled. "I can't argue with that."

She looked at some of the dresses over Margie's shoulder, but she was mostly focused on the view around them. Ferry rides went by too quickly, and this one was no exception. Margie and Lucy had hardly had time to argue about the different dresses before they had to pile into the minivan and drive onto the mainland.

Traffic wasn't bad on the way to Bellingham, and they arrived at the bridal shop just before eleven. It was stationed in an old factory that had been converted into a store, and the decor was much less stuffy than what Claire had imagined. The ceilings were at least twenty feet tall, and the walls were all exposed brick. There were multiple open rooms holding dresses of different styles, all neatly hanging on racks, and spaced evenly so as to not look overcrowded.

When they arrived, Becca popped out from behind a display dress. "This is so fun!" she said, all smiles, pulling Claire in for a hug.

"Thank you for coming!" Claire squeezed her tight. They had been reunited for just over a year, but it felt simultaneously like Becca had been gone forever and never gone at all. That was the trick with love – it made time feel infinite.

As instructed, Becca had gotten the saleswoman to pull several of the dresses Lucy had pre-selected. They were quickly escorted to a private fitting room with pink velvet chairs and a wall of mirrors.

If only she could find a way to avoid gaping at herself in all those mirrors...

The saleswoman showed her behind the curtain of a dressing room. "Would you like me to stay and help, or do you prefer to try the dresses on in private?"

Claire would rather risk having to pay for burst buttons and ripped tulle than get undressed in front of a stranger. "I'll be fine on my own, thank you."

The first dress was a structured ball gown with boning at the waist. The lace neckline came up to her throat, dotted with tiny crystals, and flared out at the shoulder.

Claire felt like a fancy lampshade. She shuffled out of the dressing room and Becca helped zip the back of the dress.

"You look like Cinderella," Lucy said, hands over her mouth.

"Or like her evil stepmother," Claire said.

"You'll match Chip, our future not-so-evil stepfather," Lucy said, cracking herself up.

Margie let out a whooping laugh, and Becca stood with her hands on her hips, shaking her head. "We're too old for this kind of look, sis."

Lillian gasped. "You're not old!"

"She didn't say we're old," Claire countered, swaying from side to side as the dress brushed the ground. "But I agree. I'm not the market for this particular gown."

Lucy stood and placed her hands on Claire's hips. "Aunt Becca brings up an interesting point." She bunched the fabric with her hands. "We essentially have two of you, Claire, so if

Becca tries on dresses, we can get through this twice as fast and not be late to our next appointment."

Becca was already backing away, eyes wide. "I don't think that's a good idea."

Claire liked the idea of sharing the burden of getting through all of these dresses. "Come on, it'll be fun."

"It's bad luck," Becca protested.

"What good is it having an identical twin if I can't use her as a living mannequin?"

Margie was already on it, rushing behind Becca and pushing her toward the dressing room. "Off we go, it's what the bride wants. You don't upset the bride, do you?"

"If only Chip had an identical twin brother," Becca mused. "Then I could marry him and we could really complete the set."

Claire laughed. "If only."

They managed to get through all fifteen of Lucy's choices in an hour.

Claire was tickled. She didn't like any of the dresses, and the prices were outrageous, but overall, shopping was going much better than the impromptu bachelorette party Margie had taken her on.

Poor Margie. It wasn't her fault that it had all gone awry. They'd gone on a trip to Utah to ski, and that was lovely – nights by the fire, drinking hot chocolate, and staying up into the wee hours talking. On the way home, however, a massive snowstorm had trapped them in Eastern Oregon for a night. Their GPS wasn't working and they nearly ran out of gas before stumbling on a Best Western. Margie fondly referred to it as "the night I almost killed all of us on the Oregon Trail."

As Claire changed out of the last dress, Lillian announced, "I'm getting hungry. Where are we going to lunch?"

Becca agreed that she was ready to eat, but Lucy insisted there was no time in their schedule. "Margie, didn't you pack sandwiches or something?"

Margie clutched her purse to her chest. "I didn't know you wanted me to pack lunch! I would've been happy to."

"I just assume you always have full catering in there," Lucy said, poking at her bag.

Claire, feeling much lighter in her regular clothes, pulled Lucy away. "We do not need to eat sandwiches out of Margie's purse. I'm treating you all to lunch."

Lucy groaned. "But we need to find you the right dress!"

"I'm sure I'll find something. If not, I'll wear a dress I already have."

Lucy stopped dead in her tracks. "*Wear something you already have*? Claire, you are the premier hotelier of Orcas Island. You can't show up at the event of the season in some ten-year-old rag you wore to Uncle Burt's wedding."

How did Lucy know she was thinking of wearing that dress? "Why not?"

"Let's get her some food," Lucy said, grabbing Claire by the arm. "She's talking crazy talk."

They piled back into the minivan and found an Italian place with an outdoor patio. After being seated, they ordered appetizers, and Margie and Lucy debated the merits of tea-length dresses.

Claire sat back and enjoyed the banter. Once their bread-sticks arrived, however, she realized Lillian hadn't spoken a word.

"Is everything okay?"

"Yes," Lillian said brightly. "Everything's great."

Lucy stopped what she was doing and shot a look at them both. "You didn't tell her?"

"Tell me what?"

Lillian shifted in her seat. "It's nothing."

"Now you have to tell us," Margie said, shaking her head. "Or we'll get very worried."

Lillian laughed. "You already seem very worried."

"Well," Margie set her water down. "I am a worrier."

"I'll tell them." Lucy leaned in, eyes bright. She cleared her throat. "Her ex-boyfriend showed up at the hotel."

"What?" Claire turned to Lillian. "Why didn't you tell me about this?"

Lillian shook her head. "I didn't know he was coming."

"He says he's going to win her back," Lucy continued, breaking a breadstick and stuffing a bit in her mouth. "But she won't have him."

Claire smiled. Once Lillian made up her mind, it was impossible to change it. This wasn't anything to worry about. Mason wouldn't be able to weasel his way back into her life, though he could make things awkward for a while.

Lillian sat back. "That's not my only issue, is it, Lucy?"

"I'm not sure what you mean," Lucy said airily.

"Go ahead. Tell Mom what you did."

Lucy shrugged, her face flat and innocent. "I don't know why you're attacking me."

"Fine, I'll tell them." Lillian straightened in her seat and folded her hands in front of her. "Lucy invited my other ex-boyfriend to stay at the hotel."

Claire couldn't stop herself. Her mouth popped open in surprise. "Dustin?"

Lillian nodded.

"Where was I during all of this?" Claire asked.

Lucy was shrinking in her seat now, trying to disappear and doing a poor job of it. "You were probably busy looking at decorations for your bridal shower."

Claire tilted her head to the side. "What bridal shower?"

Margie reached over and patted Lucy on the shoulder. "Oh honey, what are you talking about?"

"Yeah, Lucy, what are you talking about?" Becca asked, grinning.

She turned, eyes narrowed. "The bridal shower. You told me to get you a list of –"

Margie clapped a hand over Lucy's mouth. "Isn't she just the most darling when she's quiet?"

The pair of them were worse than two scheming squirrels. "Margie, did you plan a bridal shower without telling me?"

"Does that sound like something I would do?"

Lillian and Claire answered at the same time. "Yes."

She let out a small squeal. "I did! I'm sorry, but I'm also not sorry, because I managed to book that catering company you really like and I'm going to set up the hotel so nicely!"

Another event where she'd be the center of attention.

"I just want it to be magical for you!" Margie rushed. "You have so many friends in the community, and so does Chip, and they want to show their support. Everyone loves a wedding!"

She stared at them. Margie was looking at her eagerly. Becca was stuffing breadsticks into her mouth, hiding a smile, and Lucy had pink cheeks. It seemed the only one who hadn't been in on it was Lillian. She was still glaring at Lucy.

Claire took a sip of water, then set the glass down. "I'm going to need another dress," she finally said.

"That's the spirit!" Lucy sprung up in her seat, clapping her hands together.

"You're not off the hook yet, missy," Claire said, pointing at her. "Why are you inviting all of Lillian's ex-boyfriends to the hotel?"

"I only invited Dustin!" Lucy protested. "And only because he's doing that show and they booked all the rooms at the hotel. We needed the business."

Claire didn't believe her, but there was no use in arguing it now.

"It's fine," Lillian said. "Mason is fine. Dustin is fine. He's here shooting a show."

"What about you?" Claire asked.

"I'll be helping out where I can. I'm fine."

Lucy nodded. "Sounds like it's all fine."

"Do you still have feelings for this Dustin?" Margie asked.

Claire wanted to kick her under the table, but she couldn't be sure where it would land.

Lillian answered promptly. "No, of course not. He's a hot shot now, anyway." She picked up a breadstick. "It's not a big deal. It's just more of Lucy's meddling."

Everyone laughed, and then Lillian changed the subject to a vintage dress shop she'd heard about in Seattle.

Claire detected a hint of sadness in her voice, but she didn't want to push it. Lillian was never open about her love life – not even when she was dating Dustin in high school. Only recently did she start talking more about how her relationship with Mason had gone downhill.

As for Dustin, Claire lived with her own theories and guesses about what went wrong. Perhaps his proposal had scared her off? They were so young, and Lillian was never a risk taker like Lucy. Lillian was more careful, more methodical.

Did she still have feelings for him, though? Did she regret turning him down years ago? Lillian had never said anything of the sort, but that didn't mean much.

Claire's heart ached for her. Had her sweet Lillian been heartbroken all this time? If only she could do something to help.

She looked up from her plate and saw Lucy staring at her. Claire raised her eyebrows, and then, when no one else was looking, Lucy winked.

Claire had to stop herself from laughing out loud. Poor Lillian was going to have her hands full with this one.

Chapter Eight

They got back to the island late on Monday evening. Lillian had the creeping feeling that there might be more surprises waiting for her when she got home, but luckily, all was quiet.

Mason had disappeared without a trace, and Dustin hadn't been in touch at all. Had he even put her number in his phone?

Probably not. Or she was probably one of half a dozen Lillians.

Before going to bed, she checked in with Gunther to make sure he didn't need anything. He responded to her text within minutes.

"Doing great for now. Thanks for your help with the lab."

For the rest of the week, she checked in each morning and every time, Gunther thanked her and said he didn't need anything.

By Thursday, Lillian was starting to wonder if she should be more proactive and suggest island highlights for the show. She reasoned she wasn't being much of a liaison if she just sat around all day.

Was there an element of wanting to see Dustin? Sure, of course there was. She was only human. It would be nice to catch up, or even to explain that she wasn't a serial proposal-refuser, as he probably thought.

On the other hand, it was none of her business what Dustin thought of her. She kept repeating this, trying to convince herself to believe it. It was vain for her to worry about what he thought of her, because most likely he wasn't thinking of her at all.

At the same time, how could he have stood there while Mason pleaded with her and thought nothing? How could he not think she was some cruel woman who went around breaking hearts?

It was a misunderstanding. Mason might be nursing a broken heart, but he'd had more than a dozen chances to save their relationship. He'd refused to listen to her and he was unable to see anything but his own needs. After seven years together, Lillian had finally accepted that Mason was incapable of change, simply because he didn't *want* to change.

It was different with Dustin. He hadn't deserved to have his heart broken. They were so young then, though, and she didn't know what she was doing.

She thought she had been protecting him. She was certain staying with him would ruin his future, and she'd drag him down with her at some branch campus where she'd been wait-listed.

It had only taken a decade, but Lillian could admit that she hadn't been the best communicator. It wasn't an excuse, though. She'd allowed her shame to push him away, and no matter how young they were, it was wrong.

Maybe she was a cruel heartbreaker after all.

Still. She wasn't going to allow her renewed embarrassment get in the way of helping Gunther with the production. Dustin clearly wasn't holding a grudge. He hardly noticed her at all.

After finishing work early on Thursday, Lillian decided to drop by the hotel and talk to Gunther in person. If she talked to him, she could figure out what he was looking for and actually provide it.

She was halfway to the hotel when her phone rang. Lillian did a double take when she saw who it was. "Hello?"

"Hi Lillian, it's Gunther. How are you?"

"I'm good! How are you? How's the show coming?"

"We're doing very well, thank you. I hate to do this to you on short notice, but would you be available today for some scouting?"

Try not to sound too eager. "I am free today, actually."

"Wonderful. I feel like a local eye will be a huge help. Ariel can meet you in the lobby and explain what we're looking for."

Just Ariel. Her heart, the traitor, sunk in her chest. "I'll be there. See you soon."

"Great. I'll let her know."

Within minutes, she made it to the hotel and parked her car. When she walked into the lobby, she scanned the room, trying to keep her gaze casual. She spotted Ariel sitting at the hotel bar.

"Hey!" she said.

Ariel turned around, a bright smile on her face and a mug topped with whipped cream in her hand. "Lillian, thanks so much for meeting me. I am in *desperate* need of an island expert."

Now would not be a good time to tell Ariel she had only moved to the island a few weeks ago. "I'm all yours! What are we looking for today?"

"Gunther told me to 'find the orcas.' So...however we can best go about that." She laughed, and Lillian echoed her, forcing a laugh too.

"I can definitely help with that. The hotel has partnerships with some of the whale watching tours that launch from the island."

Ariel let out a puff of air. "That's a relief. I tried calling a few but no one answered. Do people not answer their phones here?"

"Well..." Lillian made a face. "You've heard of island time, right?"

"Yeah."

"I like to joke we have island technology, too. People just aren't tied to their phones or computers."

"Nice for them, stinks for me," Ariel said.

Lillian nodded. "Yeah. Give me a second. I'll grab our contacts' names from the front desk and then we can head out and meet with them in person."

"Perfect!"

Gigi was working the front desk and begrudgingly agreed to let Lillian copy the information about the whale watching tours. Once finished, she thanked Gigi and tucked the paper into her pocket.

As she walked back to the bar, her heart dropped. Dustin was there, talking to Ariel. His back was turned, so he didn't see her, and she briefly thought of fleeing.

That seemed like the cruel heartbreaker thing to do, though, so she kept walking.

"Hey," she said once she reached them. "I've got the list."

Dustin turned. He was dressed in an athletic t-shirt, the silky-looking fabric draped perfectly over his lean, muscular arms. "Hey, thanks for helping out, Lillian."

Her traitorous heart fluttered. "Ha, don't thank me until we find what you guys are looking for."

Ariel hopped from the bar stool and took the paper from Lillian's outstretched hand. "This is awesome! Why wasn't any of this information online?"

She shrugged. "Island life."

Dustin flashed a smile. "I've said it before. Lillian's the best. We're in good hands."

Her heart melted, a glowing puddle in her chest, and her breath caught and faltered. Despite wanting to answer, all she could manage was a smile.

Why was she such a sap? He was just being nice. Lillian cleared her throat. "Should we get going?"

"Sure." Ariel grabbed a large messenger bag, slinging it over her shoulder.

"Do you mind if I come along?" Dustin asked.

Lillian managed a cool shrug before turning to walk toward the doors. "Of course not. The more the merrier."

Chapter Nine

M aybe he was imagining things, but it seemed to Dustin that he was getting far nicer treatment from Lillian than Mason had gotten. She even seemed sort of happy to see him.

It didn't mean anything, of course. She'd just broken up with Mason, and in all likelihood, she was still angry with him. Maybe they were just fighting, but they'd make up and live happily ever after.

Good for her. Maybe she could make a relationship work. He certainly couldn't.

He followed Lillian through the lobby, catching himself staring at her as she talked to Ariel.

Dustin looked down, pretending to study the tile. He wasn't going to do this. He wasn't going to let himself romanticize their past. They were high school sweethearts. It was cute, but there was no reason to get all sentimental.

He'd believed in love then. He'd believed in it up until the moment his fiancée said, "We need to talk."

They walked through the doors of the hotel and into the crisp air. Lillian led them to her car, and Dustin spoke again. "I appreciate you taking the time to show us around."

"Yes, you are too nice," Ariel added. "Gunther should put you on the payroll."

Lillian laughed as she unlocked the doors to her car. "Let's see if I'm any help first."

Dustin opened the door to the backseat. It was a Nissan, at least a decade old, rusting along the bottom of the body and paint fading from the hood. The inside of the car, however, was impeccably clean and smelled of Lillian's sweet perfume.

It wasn't the roomiest car, though. Dustin squished himself into the backseat, tugging at the seat belt. "I hope this isn't getting you into trouble at work."

Lillian answered without turning around. "It's no problem. I work from home, so I make my own hours."

"What do you do?" Ariel asked.

"I'm a social worker."

Ariel gaped at her, eyes wide. "For the hotel?"

Lillian turned to back out of her parking spot, a smile breaking at the edges of her mouth. "No, I've been working for an insurance company the past few years. I help people transition from hospital stays back to their homes – doing things like getting meals delivered, having ramps installed, or arranging rides to doctor's appointments."

"No kidding!"

She nodded. "A lot of my patients are older and don't have a lot of help. It's nice that the insurance company has resources. I'm just there to connect the dots."

Dustin's brother used to call her Saint Lillian. He insisted it was an act, and that her true colors would eventually come out.

As usual, he was wrong. If only Dustin hadn't spent so many years thinking his brother knew what he was talking about. "I hope we're not taking away time from your patients."

"No, don't worry about it!" She flashed a smile over her shoulder. "I finished early today. And I think it's so fun you're making a show on the island."

"Let me tell you more about it so you know what kind of vibe we're looking for," Ariel said. "This show will be the first in a series called Natural Islands, which is part of Gunther's new brand, Natural Biosphere. Along with the show, he's planning to promote a lifestyle – natural foods, natural supplements, and classes for natural living."

"If you can't tell, he wants to focus on things that are *natural*," Dustin quipped.

Lillian let out a peep of a laugh, but Ariel, ever focused, pressed on. "He wants to capture rugged, hidden gems, like this island."

"I think I get it, but I'm not sure how rugged any of the whale watching companies are." Lillian paused. "The boats are more built for families."

"What about a sailboat?"

"You could try that, but it can be hard to catch the whales. They can pop up out of nowhere and travel quickly."

"Well, what about more like...kayaks," Ariel said.

"Kayaks," Lillian repeated. "Yeah, people whale watch from kayaks."

"That's too tame, though. Can we launch kayaks off one of those boats, make it more rugged?"

Dustin sat back and kept his jaw clenched shut. Sadly, this was not the dumbest idea that had come out of planning for the show. He didn't know how to address it, so like usual, he just kept quiet.

Luckily, Lillian handled it with grace. "Hm. I'm not sure. Let's see what the tour guide thinks. The first place is just up ahead, and they have the best ships."

They drove down a long, rocky driveway, winding through trees and low growing ferns until they reached a small cabin at the edge of the water. Just behind it, four white and black ships bobbed at a dock.

"Full disclosure," Lillian said as she got out of the car, "I just moved here a few weeks ago, so I don't know everyone as well as Lucy or my mom does."

"Oh." Ariel pulled a stack of papers and a clipboard from her bag. "Maybe we can work with them instead?"

Dustin had nothing against Lucy, but he wasn't going to spend the day with her when he could hang out with Lillian. "I'm sure Lillian's got it covered," he said.

She shot a small smile at him before walking up the wooden steps and opening the door to the building. "Hello!" she called out, walking in.

Dustin and Ariel followed, crowding the small space. The little shop was sprinkled with souvenirs and trinkets for sale – stuffed orca and seal plushies, island-themed t-shirts, rolls of nautical maps. A rosy-cheeked woman stood behind a small glass counter, and she looked up from her crossword when she saw them. "Hi there!"

"Hi, I'm Lillian. My mom Claire owns The Grand Madrona Hotel."

"Of course! I remember you from the fundraiser for Grindstone. How are you, hun?"

Lillian's expression brightened. "I'm great! We have some guests staying at the hotel who are shooting a nature show, and we're hoping to find a company to take them out whale watching for one of their episodes."

The woman clapped her hands together. "Oh, how exciting. Is this for National Geographic?"

Ariel shook her head. "No."

"Animal Planet?"

Dustin had gone through this conversation enough times to know it only went downhill from there. He decided to step in. "It's a newer company called Natural Biosphere. We've got this show, and some natural products, and promote natural living – I mean, a natural lifestyle." It sounded so much better when Ariel said it. He cleared his throat. "The show is going to focus on the wildlife of the islands."

"We'd like to get shots of Dustin, our host, kayaking amongst the whales. Is that something we can do with you? Maybe launch the kayaks off one of your ships?"

The woman frowned. "That would be tough."

"Could we kayak from here?" Ariel suggested.

"If you've got strong arms and weeks to float around," she said with a hearty laugh. "I'd be happy to take you out on one of our ships, but if you want to kayak, you need to go to San

Juan Island. Even then, you'll have to be lucky. The whales haven't come by much yet this year."

Dustin should've researched more about the whale's migration patterns before coming to the islands. There were a lot of things he should've researched, but it all had happened so fast.

Just another thing he'd dropped the ball on. "That's helpful. Thank you. Ariel, maybe we shoot some whale watching from a ship and do kayaks as a backup?"

She frowned, tapping a pen on her clipboard. "Gunther might not like that."

"It can happen on kayaks, but you have to be patient," the woman offered. "Talk to the folks over at the Whale Museum on San Juan, see if they've sighted whales traveling through the sound."

"There's an idea," Dustin said.

He hadn't even known there was a whale museum nearby. He was so far behind. Normally, he was on top of his work. An expert.

Now he felt like an amateur. Gunther sought him out because he'd liked his YouTube channel, but would his little fun videos really translate to success for this show?

The videos for his channel were easy to make. Tips about feeding a picky cat. How to trim a dog's nails. Guinea pig diets. He added a little music, a little humor, and the whole thing took off.

How had he ended up as the host of an entire nature show?

Ariel stepped forward. "If you're interested in having us film on one of your trips, maybe I can talk details with you, have you sign some paperwork and a release form?"

"Sure. No cameras on me, though!"

"That's fine!"

The woman waved a hand. "I've got an office in the back if you'd like to sit down?"

"That would be great."

They disappeared behind a wooden door, leaving Dustin and Lillian alone in the sea of souvenirs.

Lillian picked up a stuffed seal and held it next to her face. "Have you gotten to see one of these guys out on the water? They're so cute."

"Not yet," he said. Were those harbor seals? Another species to research. "Maybe we'll spot some on the whale watching episode of the show."

"How many episodes are there going to be?"

He broke eye contact, pretending to focus on a stack of seaweed-shaped pens in front of him. "We're still deciding. Gunther is, I mean. Depending on how much material we end up with."

"Oh, okay."

He turned to look at her. She was watching him with her big blue eyes, placid as the sea. Could she see right through him? Did she know how utterly unprepared he was to do any of this?

He crossed his arms over his chest and leaned back against the wall. "I might be in over my head here."

She set the seal down, its plump body rolling on the table. "I don't believe that. You were made for this."

"You sound like Gunther," he said with a laugh. "He has way too much faith in me."

"I'm sure he knows what he's doing."

Dustin said "I hope so" without thinking. He rushed to correct himself. "I mean – I really want this to work out. I need this to work. I left a job I loved at a great clinic and..."

She studied him. "Are you having second thoughts?"

He absentmindedly picked up a stuffed orca. The flippers were too small, but otherwise it was one of the most anatomically correct orca toys he'd ever seen. The eye and saddle patches were in the right places, and the tail flopped gently at the corners. "No. I just don't want to mess this up. Gunther seems to think I can talk about everything from orcas to oyster-catchers without needing a script."

"Oh, so you're telling me that you don't know everything about every animal that's ever lived?"

He suppressed a smile. "Can't say that I do."

"Then I guess you'll have to fake it 'til you make it."

"I should've known you were going to say that." He tossed the orca to her, which she caught effortlessly. "I guess...I'm just afraid that at any minute, they're going to realize I'm a fraud and kick me out."

"You're not a fraud." She took a deep breath, studying him. "To this day, you're literally one of the smartest people I know."

A laugh escaped him. "That's a shame, because the truth is, I'm an idiot."

"No you're not," she said resolutely. "And you've got friends here."

Friends. If only she knew how much he needed to hear that. "Yeah?"

"Yeah. It's understandable that you're nervous. This is something so new, but I think you're going to be great, and I'm here to help. Really. Don't be afraid to ask, okay?"

Leave it to Lillian to be so earnest. His chest swelled and he became aware, all at once, of the tension in his shoulders. Dustin relaxed the muscles and let out a breath. "Okay, I'll try to, but I don't want to bother you too much, and – well, thank you."

The end of his jumbled response was cut off when the door to the office opened and Ariel strode out. "Gunther just called. He wants us to meet him at the golf course."

"Right now?" Dustin tried to keep the disappointment out of his voice.

"Yeah. Do you mind driving us, Lillian?"

"Not at all. I'm ready when you are."

Chapter Ten

The golf course was a short ten-minute drive away. Ariel brainstormed ideas aloud and Dustin chimed in occasionally, but Lillian was too lost in thought to say a single word.

It was easy to imagine Dustin knew exactly what he was doing. He looked confident. People gravitated to him, and Gunther trusted him enough to build a show around him. Yet today, in a gift shop crowded with tchotchkes, he had opened up to her about his fears.

Lillian could see glimpses of the old Dustin – he had the same bright, dimpled smile and easy laugh – but he was decidedly grown up. He dressed more sharply, his shaggy hair had been tamed, and he projected a cool exterior that had never been there before.

Yet when he looked at her with those lost puppy dog eyes and told her he was in over his head, she'd had to force herself not to cross the room and hug him.

In that moment, he was still the same guy she'd known all those years ago: passionate, dedicated, and yes, still jumping into things headfirst without thinking.

It was on that quiet drive to the golf course that Lillian made up her mind. Maybe she couldn't make up for what she'd done all those years ago, but maybe, just *maybe*, she could still do something. If Dustin needed help to make this show a success, then Lillian was going to do everything in her power to help him.

When they got to the golf course, an employee was waiting for them in the parking lot. "I will take you to Mr. Hetch," he said.

Lillian shot a look at Dustin, and he mouthed, "That's Gunther."

"Oh," she mouthed back.

They were led to a golf cart, and Ariel, chatting endlessly, took the front seat while Lillian and Dustin took the rear. It was a tight fit, but still swanky, with cushy seats and cold water bottles perched in the cup holders.

She couldn't wait to tell Lucy about this. They'd taken a golfing trip with Rob on the mainland a few weeks ago and it had gone *very* differently. They had been rooting around in a shrub for Lucy's ball when another golfer had grabbed Lucy by the shoulder and told her that her loud mouth was "ruining the experience for everyone." This resulted in Rob shouting the guy down, then the argument boiled over, ensnaring at least five other golfers, and within twenty minutes, all of them were escorted away and asked never to return.

Compared to that, Lillian was now golf royalty. She giggled, and Dustin looked over at her. "What?"

She shook her head. "Nothing." Dropping her voice, she whispered, "I feel like we're being taken to an evil lair."

"I'm not sure we aren't," he whispered back.

The golf cart took a sharp left and Lillian teetered in her seat, bumping into Dustin's leg with her knee.

"Sorry," she said, straightening upright.

He tapped her knee for the briefest of seconds. "Don't worry about it. But try not to fall out – I don't think this guy will stop for anything."

She let out a little laugh and grabbed onto the side of her seat for more support. Gunther popped into view as they zipped over a hill, his long hair blowing in the breeze.

He wasn't alone – two other men were golfing with him. One was older, his yellow polo tucked into his high-waisted white pants. He was focused on lining up a shot.

Lillian didn't recognize the second man until the golf cart came to an abrupt halt. He turned to face them and her stomach dropped.

Mason, in a familiar golf shirt and plaid shorts.

Gunther walked over just as the older man took a whack, his ball whipping away and landing with a plop in a sand trap.

"There's our star," Gunther called out. "Dustin, I want you to meet one of our investors."

They got out of the cart as the man turned and offered a stiff smile. His blue eyes were framed with bushy white eyebrows, a stark contrast to his dark brown hair.

Did he dye his hair himself? Lillian wished Lucy were here. She liked to play a game of "bad dye job or toupee?" Lillian could hear Lucy's voice in her head, "Should've left a touch of gray for plausibility..."

She had to stifle another laugh. Luckily, no one was looking at her.

Except Mason, who was grinning like the Cheshire cat.

Ugh, why was he doing this? Lillian didn't want to keep hurting him, but how many times could she let him down gently before he realized she was serious about their relationship being over?

"Nice to meet you," Dustin said, extending a handshake.

The man nodded. "You as well."

"This is Aaron Forest," Gunther said. "He's one of the first supporters of Natural Biosphere."

Lillian couldn't decide what was worse: avoiding Mason's goofy face, or the fact that she'd now have to tell Lucy about the oil executive being involved in Gunther's nature brand.

Gunther put an arm around Dustin's shoulders. "This guy has over a million YouTube subscribers."

Aaron raised his bushy eyebrows. "And all you do is talk about animals?"

Dustin smiled, not missing a beat. "You may not know this, but the internet is powered by cat videos."

"Ha!" What might have passed for a smile crossed Aaron's face. "I think you're on to something."

"We're definitely on to something," Gunther said. "Look at this island. It's gorgeous! The viewers are going to love it."

Mason took a step forward. "Yeah, the island is pretty great. I can see why my girl wanted to move here."

His girl?

So presumptuous. And relentless! Suddenly she didn't feel quite as bad for him. "Have you ever considered she was just trying to get away from you?"

Mason smiled, undeterred.

Aaron let out a hearty chuckle. "There's an idea. Is this another one of our presenters?"

"Lillian is one of our local guides," Gunther said. "She's helping us behind the scenes."

A local guide. That was a nice way to frame her winging it. She nodded and kept her eyes fixed on Aaron.

"And Ariel, our producer," Gunther continued, "is working out a lot of the details for the show."

Aaron nodded a greeting. "Looks like you have a full crew."

"We've got some great ideas for a marine mammal episode," Ariel said. "I'm happy to tell you all about it."

"We'll catch up this evening," Gunther said. "Dustin, I want you to stick around so you can tell Aaron a bit more about our brand."

Lillian bit her lip. There was no way that Dustin didn't see the hypocrisy in all of this. Working with an oil executive on a nature show?

No, it didn't matter. She couldn't let Lucy get into her head. It wasn't like they were pumping oil into the sound. Dustin needed to impress this guy, that much was clear.

Lillian gritted her teeth and fixed a smile on her face.

Dustin seemed unaffected. "Sounds good."

"All right." Gunther clapped his hands, then pointed at the golf cart. "Away with you two. No girls on the golf course."

Lillian's eyebrows shot up. *Well, well.* That was who Gunther was, then?

Despite her best efforts, the smile slipped off Lillian's face. She shot a look at Ariel, searching for a cue. Was this how her boss always treated her?

Ariel was all smiles and forced laughter. "We're going, we're going!"

"It's technically a public course," Aaron said, standing back with his hands on the clubs. "There are no rules against women being here."

Lillian couldn't help it. She stopped her slow walk to the golf cart. "Are there actually golf courses that don't allow women?"

"Yeah. You'd be surprised," Ariel said, gently grabbing her by the arm.

"Hate to see you go, but love to watch you leave!" Mason yelled.

Lillian shut her eyes and let out a sigh. He was acting like a little brother who had tagged along for a big day out.

It was best not to show her annoyance with the whole thing. It didn't matter. Dustin had to deal with the lot of them, not her.

She kept walking, avoiding Mason and instead casting a glance at Dustin. Her heart sank when she saw him standing to the side, arms crossed and a scowl on his face.

"That wasn't cool, man," Dustin said.

Lillian froze. She regretted her annoyance. The whole thing was silly, and Dustin wasn't going to win any points by being on their side.

"Lighten up," Mason said. "I'm kidding."

Such a little brother thing to say. Lillian shot a glare at him and his goofy smile wavered, but only for a moment.

"I'm not talking to you," Dustin said, eyes focused on Gunther.

Gunther let out a sigh. "You're right, I'm sorry. That was a poorly thought out and badly delivered joke. I'm not that kind of a guy, ladies. You're welcome to stay, of course. Please stay."

"No, it's fine," Ariel said, again pulling Lillian along with her. "I've got a ton of work to do. I'll be ready to talk later."

"Thank you, Ariel. I really value your work. You're incredible, you know that?"

She beamed. "I do! Take care!"

Gunther turned away, muttering something to Aaron, with Mason leaning in awkwardly from the side.

Lillian took her seat and stole one last look at Dustin. He stood apart from the group, mouth turned down and arms still crossed. Then the golf cart took off with a jump and she lost sight of him.

As much as she'd appreciated his chivalry, she was more concerned with him torpedoing this whole project before it could begin. She was thinking of texting him to perk up when Ariel turned around and started talking.

"I do think that was just a dumb joke from Gunther. I hope you're not upset."

Lillian shook her head. "I'm not upset if you're not upset."

"Nah." She rolled her eyes. "I've heard much worse. Gunther is honestly one of the best executive producers I've worked with. Really. He's a nice guy."

"That's good."

"And Dustin," she continued, "is a total sweetheart. Don't you think?"

"Yeah." She smiled to herself. "I'd say he is."

Chapter Eleven

It was impossible for Dustin to rejoin the group and act as if nothing had happened. He was a world-class seether, and his doubts about his ability to do the show were now morphing into doubts about his desire to do the show.

He spent the next ten minutes not speaking to anyone, debating if it was time to call it quits. While Aaron was busy regaling Mason with a story about how he'd played out of a bunker on some course in California, Gunther took the chance to pull Dustin aside.

"I'm glad you felt comfortable enough to correct me," he said. "We're a team, you know. All of us."

Dustin looked at him, then back out on the fairway. "Okay."

"No, really. I was out of line. Sometimes I try too hard to be funny. Luckily, Ariel gets that."

"They're big girls. They don't need you to defend them," Mason added, sauntering over with a golf club slung over his shoulder.

Dustin clenched his teeth. It had nothing to do with Ariel and Lillian being "big girls." Gunther had dismissed Ariel like she was a dog – and Lillian, too. It was wrong.

Mason continued. "Lillian can stand up for herself. She's no angel, believe me. She's making me jump through some hoops right now."

Aaron, oblivious to any world other than his own, yelled over to them. "Only birdies over here!"

"Amazing," Gunther yelled back before turning and making a face at Dustin.

Mason ran off to Aaron's side, and Gunther dropped his voice. "I have no idea what that means. I hate golf. This whole thing makes me feel like a fraud, but he's the biggest investor we have."

Dustin could feel his frost toward Gunther thawing. It was true that Gunther could be a bit of a try-hard, but perhaps he wasn't a villain.

Dustin's phone vibrated in his pocket. "I'm with you on the golf. Excuse me, I think I'm getting a call."

He stepped away and saw that it wasn't a call, but a text from Lillian. "Don't worry about Gunther. Ariel likes him and took no offense to him being rude."

He smiled to himself. So she had seen how rude it was, too. He wasn't imagining it.

"And you?" he texted back. "Are you offended?"

"No, I'm not offended that the evil lair is boys-only. Good luck impressing Aaron. Knock his toupee off!"

Dustin cracked up and looked at the trio of boys, as Lillian had aptly called them. Gunther was standing next to Aaron and Mason, clumsily swaying a club back and forth. Mason was talking too much, and Aaron was staring off in the distance.

Some evil lair he'd gotten himself admitted into.

He typed out a response. "It makes me want to rethink this whole thing."

Lillian wrote back in seconds. "No!" Then, a moment later, she added, "Don't try to sabotage this because you're scared. What did Oscar Wilde write? Each man kills the thing he loves?"

Leave it to Lillian to quote poetry. He was grinning. "Yes, I think that's it."

"Well don't do that," she wrote. "I'm going to find some marine biologists to help you with planning. Talk to you soon."

Don't sabotage this because you're scared.

He slipped his phone back into his pocket. Lillian knew him too well, or perhaps she'd just read enough poetry that she understood human nature.

Either way, the promise of her help was enough to keep him from sabotaging himself. At least for now. And, as gross as it felt, it was time to go and try to woo the investor.

He rejoined the group to find Mason in the middle of a soliloquy about his company and work ethic.

"Now, going into the third quarter of last year, we were really aiming for that sweet spot, that eighteen percent increase. When I was in charge of my own team, we are able to leverage our partnerships to build on what we already had."

Dustin forced himself to be polite, to listen and nod along. It was painful, as it seemed like Mason was reading the index of a business textbook. He spouted dozens of words without ever actually saying anything.

It was torture, but Aaron seemed to enjoy it, and even responded to Mason with his own dense prose, parroting back some of the phrases. Gunther and Dustin followed them around the golf course like mimes, going through the motions of golfing and pretending to be involved.

Mercifully, they reached the last hole before Mason had time to tell them all about his thrilling fourth quarter. Aaron took his final shot before thanking Gunther for "a great day with great company."

"I really liked talking shop today," Mason added, shaking Aaron's hand.

"I look forward to seeing more of you," Aaron said, nodding solemnly. "You're a real go-getter. I've got to run, but I'll see you next week?"

"You bet," Mason said, waving him off.

As annoying as Mason had been, at least he'd gotten Dustin off the hook. The three of them made their way back to the parking lot and Mason suggested they go in search of "the nineteenth hole."

"Where's that?" Gunther asked.

Mason jabbed him in the shoulder. "You don't know? It means going for a drink afterwards."

"Ah, we can't." Gunther shook his head. "We need to get back to work."

"How about we get a selfie?" Mason pulled his phone out of his back pocket. "I can hype the show on my Instagram."

Dustin would rather get run over by a golf cart, but Gunther had already leaned over. "Get in here, Dustin."

He forced a smile and Mason snapped a picture of the three of them, the golf course in the background. "Cool cool. Have a good rest of your day."

"You too!" Gunther said before walking off.

Once they were safely inside Gunther's car, Dustin turned and said, "Is it me, or is Mason insufferable?"

"Oh yeah, he's the worst."

They both started laughing, and Gunther continued, "But Aaron likes talking to him, and I like keeping Aaron happy."

"This is rough, man."

"I know. That's the reality of business." Gunther pulled out of the parking spot, and within moments, Mason cut them off at the exit. He waved, smiling at Mason to go ahead. "We've got to bow and scrape to guys like that so we can do what we want to do. If it weren't for Aaron, we would've had to scrap this production already."

"What? Really?" Dustin rubbed his face in his hands. That wasn't the news he wanted to hear. "I had no idea."

"I didn't want to stress out the crew, but yeah. This show isn't cheap. But don't worry, we're set, at least for now. We can get back to work and focus on what matters."

Dustin nodded, and Gunther fiddled with the console until music started to play. They fell into a comfortable silence, and Dustin turned to look out the window.

They drove past rolling fields and little farms, stands for blueberries and hutches with huddled sheep. The houses ranged from cozy-looking cabins to sprawling villas, and though the scenery was stunning, it wasn't enough to get Dustin away from his thoughts.

The truth was, it wasn't Aaron who bothered him. He'd hardly spoken, focusing mainly on the game at hand.

Aaron wasn't the problem. Lillian hadn't dated Aaron, and it wasn't Aaron who was trying to get her back.

That was all Mason.

Dustin knew it was none of his business, but he couldn't bear to think of Lillian getting back with that tool. She deserved better. He couldn't tell her that without seeming like he was jealous, but maybe if he stuck around, he could help her see it.

Yeah. There was a reason not to quit the show. He could make sure Lillian didn't get worn down by that blowhard.

That was reason enough for now.

Chapter Twelve

It was hard for Lillian to decide who had annoyed her more: Lucy or Mason.

Mason was, at least, predictable. By the time she got home, he'd sent her a text saying how great it was to see her and that he'd be back next weekend so they could "reconnect."

She tossed her phone onto the couch without answering him and went to the kitchen in search of candy. She was digging in the freezer when Lucy walked in.

"Oh, it's you," Lucy said. "I thought an angry bear had broken in."

Lillian emerged from the freezer with chocolate Easter eggs in hand. "You weren't saving these, were you?"

"They're all yours."

She took a seat at the kitchen island, tore the foil from the first egg, and shoved it in her mouth. Then she started on the next.

"Bad day at work?" Lucy asked, taking a seat next to her.

Lillian shook her head. "Mason."

"Ah." Lucy took one of the eggs and spun it in front of her. "Just tell him you don't want to talk anymore and block his number. It's my favorite method: the cold turkey breakup."

"It's not that easy," Lillian said, mouth full of chocolate. "He keeps sneaking up and being pathetic."

"You don't have to be nice to him, you know," Lucy said. "Did he show up on the island again?"

"Yeah," Lillian said, "and he referred to me as 'his' girl."

Lucy's lips curled. "Ew."

"I know." Devouring chocolate wasn't the best way to deal with her feelings about Mason. Lillian pushed the last egg away. "I don't want to bore you with it."

"I'm not bored!" Lucy sat up. "I never get to hear good gossip anymore. What happened?"

Lillian knew she couldn't keep it all to herself, and within minutes, she blabbed the entire story of her trip to the hotel, and then to the golf course.

Lucy listened quietly, then hit Lillian with a list of demands.

"You need to do a couple of things here," Lucy said. "First, you have to tell Mason never to speak to you again, then block him."

"I can't do that. I dated him for seven years, Lucy. I can't be mean like that."

"Why not? He's being mean to you."

"No, he isn't. He's being...sad. He does all of these desperate things instead of just talking to me."

She waved a hand. "You don't need to talk to him. He had plenty of time to talk to you. Seven years of talking – no, not *listening* to you. If he'd wanted to change, he'd have done it by now."

"I know, but –"

Lucy interrupted her. "No buts. If he was the right guy for you, you would've known it years ago. You don't have to keep catering to him. He's not your problem anymore."

Huh. Lillian hadn't thought about it like that. She'd spent so many years doing what Mason wanted, it was almost second nature.

Lucy was right, though. All those years when they were together, Lillian had still felt unsure about him. Whenever he'd talked about their future, she had the urge to change the subject. Her chest would get heavy, and sometimes her heart rate picked up. It took her years to recognize that feeling as dread. It wasn't how anyone should feel about the man they were going to marry.

"Fine," Lillian said.

"If there's anyone you're considering talking to, make it Dustin. I'm sure you've noticed, but he's gotten quite hot."

She had to stop herself from saying he had always been hot.

"Lucy. I'm not going to –"

"Third, you need to get closer to Gunther to figure out what this oil guy has on him. Maybe if you earn his trust, you can get better access."

Lillian raised an eyebrow. "Oh, so I should casually stalk him?"

Lucy was undeterred, lost in her own thoughts. "We could probably get a key from housekeeping and take a peek in his room. Do you know if he keeps a laptop in there?"

"I am not breaking into Gunther's room!"

"All right, whatever." Lucy sat back with a smile. "Do the other things for now; we can focus on Gunther later. Maybe Ariel will spill the beans?" Lucy waved a hand. "No, she seems dedicated."

"How do you know she's dedicated?"

"It's just her face and the way she's always chasing after them." Lucy paused. "Unless..."

Lucy had taken off on a conspiracy train, and it was probably impossible to stop her, but Lillian had to try. "Unless what? Ariel is a spy? Or she's Aaron's girlfriend? Bet you didn't think of that. How will we crack her then?"

"Ha." Lucy nodded. "She...yeah. That's funny."

Lillian frowned. "What were you going to say?"

"Nothing. It was a dumb idea."

Lillian rolled the last egg back and forth between her hands. "Everything you just said was a dumb idea."

"It was," Lucy said, cracking a smile. "Never mind."

"I'm just kidding. Don't get all offended." Lillian nudged her with her knee. "What is it?"

"Nothing."

"Come on, don't make me beg."

"All right!" Lucy let out a sigh, then shifted in her seat. "What if Ariel isn't into Gunther. What if she's into Dustin, and that's why she's so serious and dedicated?"

Lillian felt her breath catch in her throat.

Of course. Why hadn't she thought of it before? Ariel could be a dedicated professional and *also* be into Dustin. She'd called him a sweetheart, too...

Lucy cleared her throat. "I'm just getting ideas,. You know me. It's dumb."

"No, it makes sense." Lillian forced her face to remain neutral. If it wasn't Ariel, it could be any of the other beautiful women Gunther had conspicuously chosen for his crew. "Though she might be too professional for that, though."

"Yeah," Lucy rushed to add. "I think so too." She cleared her throat. "Let's focus on Gunther. You promised you'd tell me if you found anything about him. Don't forget!"

Lillian forced a smile. "I won't."

She shoved the last chocolate egg in her mouth. Of Lucy's three-point plan, Gunther was the only part she could stomach right now.

Early on Saturday morning, Lillian got a text from Ariel. "I'm sure you're super busy and have all kinds of fun plans for Memorial Day weekend, but if you have any spare time, could I borrow you and your island charm to scope out some shooting locations?"

It was generous of her to assume Lillian had plans. Lucy was off with Rob, and her mom was busy at the hotel. Without the two of them, Lillian was left to drift through her new life like a glob of seaweed.

In truth, she was delighted to be involved with the show. It was refreshing to have something of her own, and not a burden at all. With her new mission to help Dustin, she was even more motivated to be useful.

The prior evening, she'd reached out to Margie's daughter Jade. Much like her mother, Jade knew everyone, and she was thrilled to help Dustin. They'd all gone to high school together, and Jade loved the idea of the islands being highlighted on a nature show.

She knew more than a few orca experts who worked year-round, tracking and cataloging the whales. "They're allergic to self-promotion, though," Jade added, "so a little forced spotlight might be good for them." She'd promised to get back to her with names as soon as possible.

Lillian answered Ariel's text, saying she'd be happy to help, and they met in the hotel lobby an hour later. As soon as she saw Ariel, she could feel herself clamming up as Lucy's theory forced its way into her mind.

"Hi!" Lillian waved at her from across the lobby. "How are you? Nice day, isn't it?"

Ariel put a hand to her chest. "Gorgeous! I love it here."

She was wearing a white crop top, her toned stomach peeking out, and a pair of black shorts. Very Hollywood, and very pretty. Of course Dustin would like her. Who wouldn't?

"How are you?" Lillian asked again, kicking herself for asking a second time. "Are you liking the hotel?"

"I'm good, and yes! How're you?"

"Good, that's great, glad you like it here."

Stop. Talking.

Thankfully, Ariel was unfazed by Lillian's rambling and went on in her usual focused way. "Gunther wants us to take a bunch of pictures and possibly draw out a map of locations to shoot. I also need to get release forms from whoever might be involved. I'm not sure if you know the laws about filming in the public park?"

"I don't," Lillian said slowly, fixated on Ariel's perfect eye makeup.

Was that a Los Angeles thing? Lillian's makeup never seemed to go on without a fight. Eyeshadow bunched up in the creases of her eyes, and liner ended up smudged down her nose. Maybe her eyes were too watery. Or her makeup was too old. She'd stopped trying to make it look sleek a long time ago...

"Hm, okay." Ariel tapped a pen on her chin. "I'll have to figure that out."

"I can try to help with that," Lillian said, snapping herself out of her stare. "Does Gunther have you doing this all by yourself?"

"No, no. We have other members of the crew running around, too. I'm organizing it all, or at least trying to, and filling in the gaps." She paused. "Wait – we have a lawyer on call. I guess I should field that question to him."

"Yeah, there you go."

"Lillian, you're brilliant."

She hadn't done anything, but still, Lillian clung to Ariel's compliment like a life ring bobbing in the middle of the harbor.

They stayed in the lobby for fifteen minutes to plan out their locations for the day. Despite this lingering, Dustin never appeared. Lillian wanted to ask where he was, but she couldn't bring herself to do it.

Instead, they got into Ariel's car and drove. They went from Olga to Eastsound, then to Deer Harbor and back to Moran State Park. They stopped at restaurants, talked to fishermen, and hiked around Mountain Lake.

On the trail that circled around the lake, Ariel found a rope hanging from a tree. "Wouldn't it be great to get a shot of Dustin swinging into the lake from here?"

Lillian's reply of "Oh yeah!" was extremely enthusiastic and, she hoped, convincing. In reality, she thought it was a terrible idea. There was no need to give Ariel an excuse to see Dustin with his shirt off. He wouldn't like that anyway.

When they were on their way back to the hotel, Lillian got an email from Jade with a list of marine biologists and orca researchers who were interested in helping with the show. A few had even tentatively agreed to appear on camera.

She read the message to Ariel, who responded with a squeal. "You're phenomenal, Lillian, did you know that?"

The compliments were a bit too frequent to be sincere. Lillian thanked her all the same.

"Gunther wanted to start shooting in a few weeks, but we might be able to start early. I feel really good about this."

A few weeks. A few more weeks with Dustin. "Great."

When they got to the hotel, they parted ways immediately, but again Lillian lingered. She spent some time talking to her mom about wedding plans, then she found Chip and chatted with him, and even resorted to talking to Gigi at the front desk.

Still no Dustin.

She gave up, finally deciding to leave. On her drive home, her phone rang and her heart leapt. Maybe he was thinking of her too?

"Hello?"

Rose's voice came through. "Why do you sound so weird?"

Oh. "I'm in the car."

"I know, but your voice sounds weird."

Because she was hoping it was Dustin. Why did she have to explain everything to her sisters all the time? "What's up? How are you?"

"I'm terrible."

"What's going on?"

"They put me on an improvement plan." Rose let out a sob. "At work."

Lillian gasped. "They did not!"

"Yeah." Another sniffle. "I've been working like crazy. I've worked every weekend for the past two months. It's been eighty-four days since I had a day off."

"Rose! What is going on over there?"

"My boss called me in for a meeting and I thought I was going to get promoted." She blew her nose. "That's how much of a fool I am. I thought I was getting a promotion, and instead, they're putting me on improvement plan and assigning me a mentor."

"That's absurd." Lillian let out a huff. Rose was a dedicated employee. Too dedicated, actually, and constantly taken advantage of. "Why are they being like this?"

"Ever since Olivia got promoted, she's been criticizing everything I do."

Lillian let out a groan. Olivia had started a year after Rose. They had both been administrative assistants, but Olivia had always been much more cutthroat than Rose, and apparently, it had worked out in her favor. She was in charge now.

"Rose..." Lillian said slowly.

"I know. You're going to say you told me so, and that I should've quit five years ago."

Truthfully, Lillian thought she should've quit after six months at that job. It had always been toxic, and Rose seemed especially prone to being bullied.

"I'm not going to say I told you so, but maybe now is a good time to rethink what you're –"

"Shoot! Olivia is calling me. I have to go. Love you, bye."

She disconnected the call before Lillian could respond, and a moment later, Lillian's phone rang again.

Rose, always too hasty to hang up. She answered without looking at her caller ID. "Did you call back so I can tell you I love you, too?"

"That's not what I was going for," Dustin said, "but sure, let's try that."

Lillian gasped. "I'm sorry! I thought you were Rose."

Maybe it was time to throw her phone out the window. Just end it before she began.

"Unfortunately, no. Just me. How is she?"

"She's fine," Lillian said. "How are you?"

"I'm good, I'm good. I was wondering if you had any time this week to show me around some of the beaches on the island?"

"Sure!" She paused. She didn't actually know where the beaches were, but she could figure that out easily enough. "What did you have in mind?"

"I've tried looking them all up, but I was wondering which one you think is the prettiest."

"I know just the one," she lied.

"Are you free tomorrow?"

"Yeah, I think so. Wear a swimsuit!"

He laughed. "Oh, do I need to?"

Shoot, why did she say that? It was too cold to swim. It was Ariel's fault for talking about Dustin swimming in that lake. "I mean, if you want to test the waters."

Lillian cringed, gritting her teeth.

"That's a good idea," Dustin said. "Let me know what time and I'll meet you in the hotel?"

She needed to end this call before she said anything else embarrassing. "Sure, sounds good. See you then."

Phew.

She got to her apartment and, once in the parking lot, she took a deep breath. It would be fine. She needed to chill out. None of this was a big deal. She was just helping Dustin, and Ariel hadn't seen him shirtless, and if she had, it didn't matter.

Lillian was here to help, not to get in the way. She'd talk to Marty about the beaches and steer him in the right direction.

It would all be fine, just fine, and not awkward at all.

Chapter Thirteen

It wasn't a big island. Why was it so hard to casually run into Lillian?

Dustin had grown tired of waiting, and when Ariel had mentioned that she'd spent the day driving around with her, he'd felt left out.

It was an impulse to call her like that. He told himself it was for work, because Gunther tasked him with finding "the most beautiful beach on the island."

He was surprised Lillian had answered. Even more that he'd gotten an "I love you" out of her.

There was something he hadn't heard in a long time. Even if it wasn't meant for him, it was nice.

Had she really been talking to Rose, though? Or had she been on the phone with Mason, and the whole Rose thing was a cover? Maybe they'd made up and she was back to telling him how much she loved him on a regular basis.

His stomach churned. Lillian was too good for that guy – not that Dustin could be the one to tell her. It would make him seem weird and jealous when he wasn't. It was just a true injustice to the world for Lillian to be with such a twerp.

Maybe he could get Ariel to drop a hint. She had to see it. Dustin made a mental note to bring it up the next chance he had.

He was happy, at least, that Lillian had agreed to make time for him, and he reminded himself to keep his mouth shut as he made his way to the lobby the next day.

The plan was to meet beneath the chandelier. He spotted her first, wearing a summer dress that hit just above her knee. It reminded him of a sherbet, light pink with flecks of orange and yellow. She looked like summer.

"I hope your mom won't mind me borrowing some towels." He motioned to the pair of fluffy white towels slung over his shoulder.

She let out a laugh. "I was sort of joking about the swimming."

"Why?"

"There are a few lakes that we could swim in. They're chilly, but doable."

"Sounds fun."

"But," she continued, "the prettiest beach is an ocean beach."

"Ah. And how warm is the water?"

"About fifty degrees."

He couldn't back down now and look like a wimp. Dustin rubbed his hands together. "Sounds perfect."

Lillian offered to drive and Dustin found himself blabbing the entire way there. Thankfully it wasn't a long trip, and within fifteen minutes, they pulled into a small, tree-covered parking lot.

"Is this another evil lair?" he asked, looking at a small building, apparently a toilet, off to the side of the lot.

She turned to him, stony-faced. "Yes."

The wind blew, rustling the leaves above them. Though there were a few cars parked nearby, it was otherwise silent. "Looks like a good way to end up as a victim on a murder podcast."

"Are you afraid, Dr. McGuire?" Lillian shot him a smile as she dug a gym bag out of the trunk of her car.

"Always."

She took a step toward him and for a moment, he had the bizarre thought that she was going to kiss him.

Instead of kissing him, she pulled the towels off his shoulder and stuffed them into the bag. "It's a bit of a hike to get to the beach. Do you want to go the long way or the short way?"

"Let's try the short way, and take the long way back?"

"Sure." She walked past a gate marking the beginning of a trailhead. "I've got some fabulous fauna for you."

"Fabulous fauna!" He took a step, almost tripping on a root. She didn't notice. "Music to my ears."

They walked single file down the narrow trail, Lillian leading the way. Trees surrounded them and towered overhead, with sunlight streaming in wherever it could break through. Soft pine needles muffled their footsteps, and it felt like they were the only two people in the world.

Dustin liked that feeling.

He had to go and ruin the peace by talking about the different species of trees, the history of logging on the island, the breed of woodpecker commonly spotted (that they didn't spot), and finally, about the sea otters he'd read often stole from local fisherman.

Dustin continued rambling as they walked through a campground, the different sites marked with picnic tables and fire pits, until they reached the edge of a bluff.

"Ta-da!" Lillian waved a hand, unveiling the scene below.

He wanted to kick himself. He'd been talking so much that he'd hardly noticed where they were going. Directly in front of them was a wooden staircase dusted with pine needles and framed by a crooked handrail built from driftwood. .

The beach itself lay at the bottom, composed of smooth pebbles and crossed with the occasional beam of grey-white driftwood. The ocean rolled in with gentle, lapping waves, the water a brilliant, clear turquoise near the shore and a deeper blue into the bay.

He couldn't tear his eyes away. "This is stunning."

"Do you think it'll work?"

He turned to her. "It'll blow them away."

She grinned. "Awesome!"

"Shall we?"

She nodded, taking her first strides down the stairs. Dustin followed, in awe of the scene around them. They stepped onto the beach and he sunk slightly into the stones. He had full view of the beach now, and no one else was there.

"This is incredible, Lillian. Is it always this private?"

"Yeah, I think so."

Before he could think better of it, he said, "I'm half expecting Mason to pop up."

She looked at him, hesitating for a moment before breaking into a smile. "Yeah."

Shoot. He couldn't keep his mouth shut for *one* day.

A tightness spread through his chest. He needed to do something, anything, to change the topic. Divert her attention.

"Last one in the water buys dinner!"

With that, he tore off his t-shirt and took off.

Chapter Fourteen

Nope, he had not let himself go since high school, no sir, not even a little bit. His shoulders were buff, his arms were toned, and though he didn't have the try-hard sharp abs of a gym rat, he'd remained lean and fit.

Lillian realized her mouth was hanging open, so she shut it. Dustin was submerged up to his waist, holding his arms gingerly above the surface, the sun reflecting off the water and illuminating the rippling muscles of his back.

"It's not even that bad," he said, turning to face her.

She dropped the bag and walked to the edge of the water. "Oh?"

"Well, I can't feel anything." He laughed. "Are you coming?"

"It's too cold!" She slipped off her sandals and put one foot in the water. "And I never agreed to go in."

Goosebumps covered his chest. "Then you're going to owe me dinner."

"I've already lost. You ran in so fast."

He smiled. "Yeah, your reaction time was really lacking."

She took a deep breath and stepped back onto the dry stones of the beach. The sun and stones immediately began warming her skin to a normal temperature.

This wasn't the first time she'd been tempted to jump into the water surrounding the islands. At the ferry terminal, the water was so clear she could see to the sandy bottom. The blue color was alluring, too, but the only one who was ever crazy enough to go swimming was Marty.

"You know how when you get in, it feels better as you adjust?" Dustin asked.

She nodded. "Are you starting to warm up?"

"No, the opposite. I'm having a hard time breathing."

She let out a cackling laugh. "You're not really selling it, Dustin."

"It's like my muscles are giving up. Just seizing."

Truth be told, he looked fine. Robust, even. The water was blue and calm, and with the sun, how long would it even take her to recover?

She'd worn a swimsuit, after all. Deep down, she'd hoped this might happen.

Lillian pushed her sandals aside and carefully pulled her dress over her head, tossing it onto the beach.

"No, really, don't come in. It's awful," he said, putting a hand up. "I don't know why I did this, and I'm full of regret."

"I can handle it," Lillian said. She didn't really believe that, but she wanted to believe it. She wanted to be the Lillian who didn't overthink everything, who didn't hold back, who didn't live tottering along meek and half-hearted.

"Try to come in slowly, because it's rocky and –"

Lillian ran full-speed toward him, splashing into the water and sending waves into his shoulders.

Dustin yelled out and turned his head to avoid getting splashed in the face, but Lillian pressed on and waded closer.

She was a head shorter than he was, and by the time she reached him, her chest was beneath the icy water. It was the strangest sensation. Her skin burned and tingled everywhere all at once, as though being pricked by a million needles. Her lungs constricted, making it hard to breathe, and her feet were going numb.

"Refreshing!" she said with a laugh.

Dustin's teeth chattered as he spoke. "This was a bad idea and I'm sorry."

"Bad idea? Why?" She smiled before taking a deep breath and plunging beneath the water head-first.

Lillian zoomed past him, opening her eyes into the saltwater. It stung at first, but with the pain all over her body, it was hardly noticeable. The sun illuminated everything around her, and for a moment, it felt like she was floating on a cloud. A freezing, painful cloud.

She popped back to the surface and gasped in the air, her lungs stiff but very much alive.

"You're wild!" He shook his head. "I don't think I can do it. I can't."

"Come on!" she shouted. "Once your hair gets wet, you adjust better."

"Really?"

"Yeah!"

He hesitated for a moment before plunging straight into the water. He emerged a moment later, wiping at his eyes. "You lied!" he yelled.

Lillian laughed. She'd grown familiar with the pain across her skin. It hadn't improved, but she could tolerate it. She dove back down and swam toward him. By the time she made it, he was nearly out of the water.

"I'm done. I can't handle it," he said, dabbing a towel to his face. "I don't know how you can stand it."

In the shallow water near the shore, the sun had warmed the water by a few merciful degrees. Lillian launched herself backwards into the water. "I didn't realize I hadn't *lived* until now!"

"Maybe you should be the one doing Gunther's show." Dustin laughed. "Because he's definitely going to make me get in the water a dozen times, and I think I'll quit on the spot."

She stood, poking at her numb leg with one of her fingers. "Ah yes, heavy lies the head that wears Gunther's natural crown."

He cracked a smile. "The crown made of seaweed."

She dove back underwater, thrilled by the feeling of her body floating so freely. When was the last time she'd gone swimming? It had been years, and even then, swimming in a pool was so different. It was confined. Here, she felt infinite.

She popped back up and Dustin called out to her.

"C'mon, it's time to get out," he said. "You're going to get hypothermia and I'll have to run in to save you."

"Aw, you'd save me?" It was more difficult to catch her breath now, but she was determined to stay in the water, as it seemed to be getting a reaction out of him.

"Yes. Now please get out before you force me into being a hero."

She wanted to say something sassy back to him, but her breathing was shallow and she could hardly form an "Okay."

When she walked out of the water, he wrapped a towel around her shoulders. "Remind me to never dare you to do anything again."

The muscles on her face were stiff and it hurt to smile, but she couldn't stop herself. "I had to try to win that dinner back."

His hands lingered on her shoulders for just a moment before breaking away. "Clearly. Well, you've earned it. We never would've found this place without you."

"And the viewers won't have to feel how cold the water is."

"Hopefully I won't have to, either." He grinned at her. "Thanks, Lillian. This has been – it's just amazing."

"You're welcome. It's an amazing place. The whole island, really."

"Yeah." He took a step back and cleared his throat, looking over the water. "What made you decide to move here?"

She took a shaky breath. Her body wasn't warming up as quickly as she'd hoped. Sunlight might help, but out of the water, she'd lost her boldness. She wasn't going to stand in front of him in her swimsuit. "I wanted to be near family. And..." *How to put this?* "I needed a change."

Their eyes met and she looked away, pretending to study the horizon.

Dustin cleared his throat. "Whatever the reason, I'm happy for you. You seem..."

She turned back to look at him, cutting him off. "Unbalanced?"

He laughed. "No. You seem different."

"Yeah, I guess I am. You're different, too, you know. You've grown up."

A drop of water slipped from his hair and fell into his eye. He squinted, a boyish smile flashing across his face. "It's like I had this image in my head of high school Lillian. Obviously I knew you'd changed, but I couldn't imagine how."

"That bad, huh?"

"No." He took a deep breath, suppressing a smile. "I couldn't imagine how you could get any cooler, but you did."

"It's the water." She turned her head again, watching a large white yacht glide past in the distance. "It iced you out, too."

He laughed. "I guess you're not that different. You still can't take a compliment."

Still facing away, she smiled to herself. "And you still think to yourself out loud."

"I do, don't I?" He paused. "It's just nice being here with you, and –"

The muffled sound of a phone rang out, and he stopped, jogging back to the staircase where he'd dumped his belongings on the ground.

Lillian had to force herself to stop gawking and instead face the sea.

It was better he didn't finish that statement. And best she didn't read too much into his comments.

Easier said than done, of course.

Chapter Fifteen

It was lucky his phone rang. He'd gotten too caught up in the moment.

It was this beach. It was too picturesque, too tranquil. Too magical. Or maybe the cold water had stunned him.

"Hello?" Dustin looked up. Lillian was sitting on the driftwood log with her back to him. He could see her head tilted upwards, facing the sun.

She was cool, though. He meant what he'd said, and luckily, he hadn't gone on to tell her any more. She looked so happy and free, so stunning...

"Where are you?" Ariel whispered. "We're all waiting for you to talk about this beach segment."

"Oh, sorry. I'm just heading back."

"Did something happen?"

Other than him being a desperate fool who couldn't keep a relationship going to save his life, but also couldn't keep himself away from his ex?

"No. It's sort of a hike to get here."

Ariel was quiet for a moment. "Weird. Okay, I'll talk about the lakes and hopefully you'll be here when I'm done."

"Yeah, definitely. Thanks."

He stooped down and picked up his wallet before jogging over to Lillian.

"Everything okay?" she asked.

"Yeah. I just need to get back to the hotel. They're waiting for me to talk about this part of the shoot."

She stood and grabbed her dress from the stones. For a moment, he had the urge to call Ariel back and cancel the whole thing. Then he and Lillian could spend the day at this beach, watching the water, waiting for whales and otters to join them in their revelry.

It was a silly thought. He turned to give Lillian privacy as she got dressed, then they both rushed up the stairs, passing under the tree cover into the cool forest.

Without the sun, his skin chilled within minutes, and goosebumps prickled on his arms. They walked quickly, however, and soon the sustained movement warmed and relaxed his muscles.

Twice he nearly toppled to the ground, tripping over unseen rocks and roots, while Lillian glided across the trail ahead of him like a ballerina. She wasn't even wearing real shoes, just a pair of flimsy sandals. How did she do it?

Back in the car, he felt he could speak without embarrassing himself. "Should I pick the restaurant, or would you like to?"

She seemed to think on this for a moment before answering. "I'll pick. When are you free?"

He frowned. "I'm not sure. Gunther decided we shouldn't wait to start shooting, so the plan is to start filming this week."

"Ah. You're very busy and important, then."

He laughed. "No. I just need to check with Ariel and I'll get back to you."

"Works for me."

She dropped him off outside the hotel and he rushed up to Ariel's room, where the planning meeting was in full swing.

"I've got the best beach," he said breathlessly when he burst through the door. "Though – don't kill me – I forgot to take a picture."

It was decided they'd start shooting the next week with one of the wildlife experts Lillian had found. Gunther wanted B roll of them walking, talking, and looking at various island animals and landscapes.

Dustin didn't know how it would all fit together, but he wasn't asking questions. In fact, the less involved he was, the better. He recognized he was out of his depth. Though he knew about animals and how to keep people engaged for a few minutes at a time, making an entire show was beyond his expertise.

On top of that, the whole process was exhausting. Ariel and Gunther had boundless energy to bicker. They could, and did, argue into the wee hours of the morning as the director, production designer, and technical director hammered out the actual plans.

For Gunther and Ariel, no detail was too small, no argument too petty. The most recent debate was on dramatic narratives in documentaries. Gunther wanted to weave a story about a seal in the harbor, starting with how adorable it was, talking about its family, where it ate, how it slept, then BAM! Show it being eaten by an orca.

Ariel thought that was off-brand, and besides, she argued, they needed to focus on the salmon-eating orcas, not the ones who ate porpoises and seals. Gunther wasn't aware the orcas weren't all the same, which gave Dustin a few minutes to shine as he explained the different groups before falling back into silence.

Sitting around as everyone else actually worked was giving Dustin too much time to think. He couldn't stop replaying his day with Lillian.

What had her life been like the last ten years? What was her day-to-day like at her job? Did she have a lot of work friends? Did she still like to bake? Over the years, all he'd been able to learn about her life was from pictures she'd posted online – a girls' trip with her sisters, a dog she'd met at the park. It was embarrassing that he knew all of these by heart, like he couldn't get over her a dozen years later.

He was over her, though. He didn't want to be with her. He didn't want to be with anyone. Love was a farce. A gamble. It meant handing your heart over to someone and having no control over what they did with it. It meant believing what they told you. It meant playing Russian roulette with your sanity.

Dustin was better off alone. After his fiancée had left him, he created his YouTube channel and found all those viewers. And now look where he was! He was living a dream. He was going to host his own show.

Her leaving him was the best thing that could've happened. He was thriving on his own, finally free of his romantic delusions.

These thoughts circled as he sat listening to Gunther and Ariel's increasingly raised voices.

Dustin should have known spending time with Lillian was a mistake. It was kicking up old feelings, confusing him, making him nearly forget what it was like to have his heart trampled again and again.

Away from her, though, the memories came back. He remembered how his chest had tightened when his fiancée and brother had asked to talk. He knew something was wrong, sitting there across from them, the room-filling scent of his brother's cologne burning his nose.

He remembered how dry his mouth had been when his fiancée said how sorry she was, how they'd "just fallen in love," how there was nothing he could've done differently. He remembered the cold porcelain of the toilet against his arms that evening as he heaved and heaved.

How could he forget?

Dustin wasn't going to go through it again, and as much fun as he'd had with Lillian that day at the beach, it needed to end there. Spending time with her was a distraction, a way for him to sabotage his own success.

"Dustin!"

He looked up. Ariel was staring at him.

"Sorry, what?"

She let out a sigh. "Do you have that segment written up on the big seals that live around here?"

"Stellar sea lions, and yes. I'll email it to you."

This satisfied her, and she turned her attention back to the technical director. He pulled out his writeup on the 2,500 pound pinnipeds, deleting his long-debated title "A Ton of Fun" at the last moment before hitting send.

There. That was done. Back at work, doing what he needed to be doing.

He'd made up his mind. Dinner with Lillian was off the table. It was silly that he'd even suggested it. He was being competitive, an in-the-moment kind of thing. A joke, really. She wouldn't care if they didn't actually go out for a meal. Lillian had wasted enough of her time on this production.

He wasn't going to bug her anymore. In fact, if he didn't see her again before he left, that would be for the best.

Dustin pulled out his phone and typed a message. "Hey, things are picking up with the show. We're going to start filming soon. Don't think I'll have time for dinner. You're off the hook. Thanks for your help, and good luck with everything."

Chapter Sixteen

Lucy wanted – no, *needed* – to tell Lillian about Gunther, but the timing was impossible. For Lillian to take it well, she had to be in a good mood, and Lillian hadn't been in a good mood in two weeks.

Try as she might, Lucy couldn't cheer her up. No magic number of maple lattes, surprise tacos, or cute cat pictures did the trick. Lillian's smiles were brief, her conversations were short, and for the first time ever, her evenings were filled with work.

Lucy tried asking her about what was going on, but she was met with nothing but denials.

"You don't seem yourself," she'd finally said to Lillian on a rainy Thursday evening.

Lillian didn't look up from her laptop screen. "Don't I?"

"Is it Dustin? Was he mean to you?"

She shook her head. "I haven't seen him. He's busy with filming."

"Is it Mason? Is he still calling and bothering you?"

"He is," she said, "but I ignore him, mostly." She looked up, then back at her screen. "Sorry, I've got to focus on this. One of my patients needs a hospital bed at home and we're having a hard time getting one."

It could just be her job. Lillian cared a lot about these people, and caring about people was stressful. Far more stressful than Lucy's job at the farm.

Whatever was going on, Lucy grew tired of waiting. She had dirt on Gunther and she needed Lillian's help to find out more. She knew he was up to something; she just wasn't sure precisely what it was.

The next night, she got home to find Lillian camped out on the couch. Sweatpants, a cheesy Christmas movie in the background, and Lillian hunched as she scrolled through her phone. Not a pretty sight.

Lucy stepped in front of the TV and announced, "I'm getting you out of this slump."

Lillian didn't even look up. "Hm?"

Unbelievable. It was like she was in a trance. Lucy snatched the phone from her hand and earned a glare from Lillian.

"Excuse me, did you just –"

"I meant what I said. I'm getting you out of the apartment. It's Friday night! C'mon, let's live a little!"

"I'm relaxing." She reached forward and took the phone back. "That's an important part of living."

Lucy let out a sigh. This wasn't going to be easy. "Listen. I get it. You made a big change in your life and you're having a hard time adjusting. That's okay, but you shouldn't wallow. You need to find a way to thrive, Lil."

"And you're here to help?" Lillian cast a smile. "Why do I feel like you're about to pitch a horrible scheme to me?"

She cringed. Busted. "Because I'm about to pitch an *exciting* scheme to you."

"No thanks." She turned back to her phone.

Lucy picked up a pillow and threw it at her.

"Hey!" Lillian pushed it aside. "I'm not interested, okay? Leave me to wallow."

"Aha! You admit it. You're wallowing."

Her chest heaved with a breath, then slowly deflated. "I'll admit I'm not thriving."

"Let me help." That was the opening she needed. Lucy crept closer. "I'm going to ask you to keep an open mind."

"What's the scheme, Lucy?"

"It's something to protect Dustin."

"Why?" Lillian put her phone down. "Did something happen?"

"I found some concerning things about Gunther."

Lillian let out a groan. "Not this again. Lucy, he's just a guy who makes you uncomfortable because he wears his hair too long and talks too much about zodiac signs."

That was true, but beside the point. "He's also a guy who started a skincare company and ruined it in record time."

Lillian sat up. "Where did you see that?"

"It took some digging, but I uncovered a company called Hetch Serums. There's not much about it online, but I found some people who tried to sue the company for causing their entire bodies to break out in hives."

"Are you sure Gunther was a part of it?"

"Yeah. Check this out." Lucy pulled out her phone, opening to a picture of one of the anti-aging serums. "This is from the lawsuit."

Lillian took the phone and zoomed in. A small, square portrait of Gunther decorated the bottle's label, smiling a bright white smile, his skin glowing and tanned.

"So he sold some bad face cream." She shrugged. "That's kind of on-brand for him."

"It wasn't just that." Lucy navigated to another website. "Here's a forum with a bunch of disgruntled former employees. Fifty-seven people he didn't pay for their last six months of work!"

"Six months!" Lillian grabbed the phone again. "Why?"

"Because after being sued, he filed for bankruptcy and said 'sorry suckers.'"

"I don't think it works that way."

Lucy scoffed. "It works that way all the time, and almost always in the boss's favor."

"You can tell Dustin about it, I guess." Lillian settled back into the couch, pulling a pillow onto her lap. "Let him decide what to do with that information."

She was being her passive self, not wanting to get involved, saying that people should make their own –

Wait a minute.

Lucy sat next to her. "Why don't you want to tell him?"

She shrugged, eyes on the TV.

Time to increase the pressure. Lucy set her phone aside. "What if Gunther is a chronic scam artist, and this time Dustin gets dragged down with him?"

Lillian turned, her eyes narrowing, her forehead creased with tension.

Good. Now she was listening.

"Dustin could get caught up in Gunther's fraud. He could be fined, maybe even go to jail."

"That's not funny, Lucy."

"I'm serious! We need to find out what Gunther is up to. I just know there's something."

There was Silence stretched out for a moment while Lillian rubbed her face with her hand, looked at her phone, then tossed it aside before looking back at Lucy.

"What's your plan?" she finally asked.

Yes!

"First, you need to find out when they're shooting tomorrow. I'll get Gunther's room key and we'll have a look around. It'll be really fast, like ten minutes. We can copy some files from his computer and review them later."

"No, Lucy, that's insane. We can't commit a crime at Mom's hotel."

"What if Gunther is currently committing crimes?"

"Then tell Chief Hank. Or tell Margie, and she'll tell Chief Hank, and he can investigate because he's actually an officer of the law."

Lucy waved a hand. "Right, because he's going to get a warrant to search Gunther's room based on my hunch and online sleuthing."

A groan erupted from Lillian, and she sprung from the couch and walked to the kitchen. "Do we have any ice cream?"

"I'll buy you some."

"No, don't, I don't want ice cream." She stopped. "Just – let me sleep on it."

Whoa.

Lucy drew herself up. No need to push any harder. That was much more progress than she had expected. She thought it would take days, maybe eons, to argue Lillian into helping her with this. Lillian was anti-shenanigans, but apparently bringing Dustin into it changed her tune.

She still loved him. He was obviously the cause of her slump, even if she wouldn't admit it.

Lucy had a feeling it was all connected. If they could figure out Gunther, then Dustin would follow. She didn't know how, but she could just feel it.

She smiled. "I'll await your answer in the morning."

Chapter Seventeen

S leep did not come easily that night. Lillian snuck off to her room and spent two hours poring over the lawsuit against Gunther's company, then another hour reading through complaints from jilted employees.

No one could deny Gunther's integrity was questionable at best. That wasn't why she couldn't sleep, though. She was worried about Dustin.

On the other hand, was it her place to worry about him? He'd ditched her for dinner and not spoken to her since. She had already run through all the possibilities – she'd offended him, he was too busy with work, he had a parade of new girl-friends and had forgotten about her – but the bottom line was, no matter the reason, he didn't care about her. Why should she care about him?

Exhausted and bleary-eyed, Lillian managed to fall asleep for a few hours before being roused by the sound of Lucy clanging pans in the kitchen. The events of the previous night drifted back to her, and Lillian tried to cover her growing dread by pulling the duvet over her eyes.

The smell of fresh coffee filtered in, and before long she gave up on sleep, pulled on her robe, and shuffled into the kitchen.

"Morning!" Lucy said brightly. She was already dressed in yoga pants and a flowing, white athletic shirt. Her hair was tied back, bouncing around as she filled a mug with coffee. "I'm making pancakes."

Lillian accepted the mug. "I thought I heard a mixer going."

"How'd you sleep? You look terrible."

Lillian laughed. "Thanks."

"Do you want eggs?"

She was trying to butter her up with breakfast. It wasn't going to work. "I'm not doing it, Lucy. I'm not breaking into Gunther's room to satisfy your paranoia."

Lucy turned and opened the fridge, pulling out a pitcher of apple juice. "I was thinking scrambled, but I can make hard boiled if you prefer."

"If Dustin gets in trouble, that's his problem. He doesn't care about me, so I don't care about him, either."

Lucy laughed and poured a glass of juice. She took a swig before turning back to the oven. "Sure."

"It's true! Why should I endanger myself by –"

Lucy cut her off. "Be honest with yourself, Lil. You care about Dustin. Maybe you don't want to, but you do."

Steam rose from the surface of Lillian's coffee. She watched the elegant dance, curving and twisting, drifting higher until it disappeared.

"It's not your fault," Lucy added. "That's who you are. You care about everybody." She returned to the fridge, grabbing a jug of pumpkin spice creamer and plopping it down. "There's no use in fighting it."

Lillian poured a dollop of cream into her mug. The plume expanded slowly, lightening as it went. "He doesn't want anything to do with me."

"Aw, I don't think that's true." She paused, a frown on her face. "Even still, do you want him to get dragged into jail with Gunther?"

It took her a moment to respond. "No."

"Are you really *that* afraid of poking around Gunther's room?" She didn't wait for a response. "I already have a plan. You'll call Ariel and tell her you have something for Gunther. A gift, as a thank you, for being an honored guest."

The pumpkin flavor was impeccable. She didn't care if it wasn't the season for pumpkin. Lillian could drink ten of these a day, though the caffeine might overload her nerves. "I'm listening."

Lucy hurried on. "Ask if they're around today, and when she hopefully says no, you can say you'll just drop the gift off in his room. There! We have a cover if anyone sees us going in or out, and we have permission to be there."

She wanted to say no, but surprisingly, it wasn't the worst idea she'd ever heard. Lillian looked up from her mug just as Lucy slipped a plate of pancakes in front of her. There were four of them, round and puffy, the centers golden-brown.

The smell of vanilla calmed her nerves. "What's this special something we're getting him?"

"I made a gift basket." She waved a hand. "Don't worry. I'll stand guard outside the room the entire time. This is going to be fun, Lillian! You'll see. We're going to find something, and probably save Dustin's life."

Lillian took a bite of pancake. Lucy had sprinkled cinnamon into the batter, just like she liked.

She was good. Too good. "It's a little too crazy for me, Lucy."

"Come on! Ten minutes. Just ten minutes, and then if we don't find anything, I promise I'll never bring it up again."

Lillian laughed, accidentally launching little bits of pancake across the kitchen island. "Yeah right."

"I swear." Lucy put a hand on her chest. "Hand over my heart, I promise I'll let it go."

She reached for the canister of whipped cream Lucy had set out, along with the maple syrup, the jam, and the bowl of blueberries.

Lucy knew how to put a spread together. The gift basket was probably gorgeous. Gunther would love it, and at the very least, it would get Lucy to shut up about this conspiracy.

Lillian topped her next pancake with a crown of cream. "Fine. Whatever. *Five* minutes."

Lucy let out a squeal. "Yes! This is going to be great."

She took another bite of pancake. The whipped cream had melted a bit, soaking in and sweetening it.

Lillian let out a sigh. It could be worse – she could be snooping around in Dustin's room.

Now that would be too far.

An hour later, after calling Ariel about the gift and confirming they were out of the hotel, Lillian found herself skirting across the third floor in The Grand Madrona Hotel.

Her view was obstructed by the ridiculously tall gift basket Lucy had put together. It was skillfully done, filled with island favorites of wine, cider, and honey, the edges padded with dried flowers and cookies, all beautifully packaged and delightfully decadent. She'd topped the basket with a red bow and wrapped it in cellophane, which now crinkled with Lillian's every step.

She told herself not to think too much about what they were doing. Gunther's room was the last door on the right, and as they made the march from the elevator to the end of the hall, they didn't hear or see anyone else.

"Okay," Lucy whispered, pulling the housekeeping key from her pocket. "I'm going to start my timer as soon as you go in. If anyone comes up, I'll knock once on the door so you can come out right away and act like you just dropped off the basket."

"Let's hope it doesn't come to that." Lillian shifted the basket. It was heavy, and her hands were slippery with sweat.

Lucy craned her neck down the hall. "I think we're good. Go!"

The lock clicked, and Lucy pushed the door open. Lillian bumped into the door with the basket before stumbling inside.

The door closed behind her and she stood for a moment, paralyzed with the reality of how irresponsible this was.

What was she thinking? It was insane. Why did she let Lucy talk her into these things?

Lillian hurried over to the desk near the window, stepping over piles of clothes and paper bags filled with takeout containers.

Apparently Gunther didn't like housekeeping in his room. The desk, too, was messy, covered in papers and folders, with a laptop sitting open at the center.

She didn't want to move the papers, as he probably wouldn't be happy to see she'd messed with his stuff. Lillian looked around the room, hoping to find an alternative place to set the basket, but every surface was covered with junk. There were piles of shirts covering the bed. The dresser had a zippered bag splayed open, vials of hair oils and containers of lotions spilling out and teetering precariously at the edge.

This was *way* too personal, being in here. She shouldn't have come in, she shouldn't have even entertained the idea. It had been less than a minute, but Lillian decided she was going to get out of here and leave the basket outside of the door.

Lillian turned, heaving the basket on her hip as the glass bottles clanked into one another. Why had Lucy picked so many liquids for this thing?

She bent to the side, steadying herself, and something caught her eye. Her brain registered it first, but she'd already taken a few steps before she became conscious of it.

Lillian stopped and turned back to look at the desk. It was the oddest thing. She could have sworn she'd seen a picture of Lucy.

That made no sense, but the thought nagged at her, and she set the basket on the floor before turning around to scan the desk.

Amongst the papers and empty coffee cups, there it was – a picture of Lucy.

Lillian picked it up. It was a printout from a news story. The headline read **Local Activist Saves Farm**. Her name was highlighted in yellow: *Lucy Woodley*.

Lillian's hands moved quickly. She grabbed the stack of folders beneath the story and opened the one on top. There were more articles about the island, some about the county council, one about a proposed desalination plant. Then an article about seismic airguns. Another picture, this one of Jade's friend Kelly from the Friday Harbor Laboratories. A business card from the Bureau of Ocean Energy Management.

She frantically flipped through the papers, trying to find a pattern or a trend, something to make it make sense.

A voice emerged behind her. "What are you doing?"

Lillian stiffened, clutching the files in her hands as she slowly turned her head. The door to the adjoining room was cracked open, and a woman with flowing blonde hair was staring at her.

"I'm dropping off a gift basket," she said, her voice breathy and weak.

"No, you're not. I just watched you go through those files."

Lillian kept her eyes fixed on the woman as she set the folder down. Caught red-handed. She couldn't even come up with a lie. "I'm sorry. I'll go."

The woman stepped in front of her. "I don't think so. I'm calling the cops."

"Please don't. This is a misunderstanding. I've been helping Gunther, and I just wanted to drop this off. I talked to Ariel."

She pulled something from her pocket and pointed it at Lillian, her hand shaking. "I will spray this mace right in your face."

Lillian promptly put her hands up in the air. "No, please —"

"Quiet! You can't be in here. You're going to my room." She kept one hand steady, then used her other hand to make a phone call. Her voice shook as she spoke. "Hi, someone is trying to rob one of our hotel rooms. Please hurry!"

Chapter Eighteen

What was taking her so long? Lucy peered down the hall, then turned back to look at her watch.

It had been twelve minutes. She must have found something. A giddy surge rippled in Lucy's chest.

She'd expected Lillian to come running out right away; she didn't have the stomach for these things. Lucy would've preferred to do the searching herself, but Lillian was the liaison. It would be harder to cover up if Lucy were the one caught in the act.

They weren't getting caught, though. The hotel was dead at this hour. Everyone was out enjoying the beautiful day. She'd need to take Lillian outside after this. Maybe there was an outdoor Pilates class they could sign up for...

The muted ding of the elevator echoed and Lucy shot her arm out faster than a bullet, hitting the door to Gunther's room with a loud, distinct knock.

Nothing.

The doors were thick. Too thick. Maybe Lillian hadn't heard her. She banged again.

Two officers stepped out of the elevator and walked toward her. Lucy didn't recognize them, and a sick feeling settled into her stomach.

"Hello gentlemen!" she called out. As the officers got closer, she added, "Er, and lady."

The woman officer nodded at her, stopping at the door next to Gunther's.

Phew. It wasn't for them. It was incredibly bad timing, but the police weren't there for them.

"San Juan County police," she called out, banging on the door. It opened and they disappeared inside.

They were playing with fire. It was way overdue for Lillian to get out of there. Lucy unlocked the door and slipped inside.

"Lillian," she whispered, "we've got to go."

The room was a mess, and it took Lucy a moment to take in her surroundings. The smell of old food lingered, and the gift basket sat on the floor near the desk.

Lillian was nowhere to be seen.

"Where are you?" she whispered, her voice raspy.

Lucy stepped over all the garbage and made her way to the bathroom at the far corner of the suite. The door was open, and it too was empty.

The only sound was coming from the adjoining room. Muffled voices, a woman's, then what sounded like a man.

Wait a minute.

She snuck back out of the room just as Lillian stepped into the hallway, her hands cuffed behind her back, her face ghostly pale.

"Wait!" Lucy called out. "Where are you taking her?"

The male officer turned around. "This one yours?"

"That's my sister."

He turned and kept walking. "You can pick her up at the county jail."

They stepped onto the elevator, spinning Lillian so she faced the front. Her lip was trembling.

Lucy wanted to think of something to say, but nothing came to her. The doors slid shut and Lillian disappeared from view.

Lucy stood, staring at her reflection in the shining metal.

This was quite possibly the worst thing Lucy had ever done. Lillian would never forgive her. Claire was going to kill her.

Who could help them out of this one? Could Marty hack his way out of it?

No, that wouldn't help. Maybe Margie – she knew everyone. Her husband Hank was the Chief Deputy Sheriff. He could help! Jade's boyfriend was a cop, too, over on San Juan Island...

She needed backup. It was time to make some calls.

Chapter Nineteen

First the patrol car, then the police boat, then another patrol car. It felt like it was happening to someone other than her, as though she were watching a movie.

Except it wasn't a movie. It was real. The twist of the handcuffs on her wrists, the crackling of the police radio, the roar of the boat's engine as they rode to San Juan Island – it was all real.

Lillian floated along, only partially aware of being booked and going through a series of questions she didn't know how to answer.

"I was dropping off a gift basket," she insisted.

"How did you get in the room? Did you steal a key?"

She shook her head. "No, I was just dropping off the basket."

The officer let out a sigh. "You seem like a nice girl. Why don't you tell me what happened? I can try to help you."

She bit her lip. "Ariel told me it was okay to drop it off."

The officer didn't spend much time with her. He was called away after only a few minutes. Lillian sat in the room, staring at a blank wall, alone with her thoughts.

She was going to be charged with a felony. She'd lose her social worker license, then she'd lose her job. Her savings would slowly disappear. The hotel's reputation would be tarnished, and her mom would have to denounce her to recover her reputation with the community. Lillian would denounce herself, actually, and flee the island to hide in a city where no one would know her shame.

Canada wasn't too far, and she'd always liked Canada. Could she emigrate as a felon?

The door opened. "Woodley?"

"Yes?"

"You're out." The officer pointed his thumb over his shoulder. "Come with me."

He handed her a bag of her belongings and she followed him through the winding hallways. When he reached the double doors leading to the lobby, he said, "Your husband bailed you out."

"My husband?"

Her heart leapt. Had Dustin come to her rescue? Had Lucy called him and explained what they'd done, and he'd talked to Gunther and cleared it up as a misunderstanding?

Lillian was so angry at herself for being so incredibly foolish, and she wasn't above begging for forgiveness. Why had she agreed to do it in the first place? She couldn't explain it; she was mystified herself.

She'd never gotten in trouble before, not even a detention in school. Lucy was the one who could handle being in trouble. She lived for it. She loved confrontation. Lillian should never have gone along with any of this.

Yet now, she had hope again. Perhaps she'd been too hasty in her despair. Her chest was getting lighter by the second. The officer pushed the doors open and she walked through, scanning the lobby for Dustin's sandy hair, her ears tuned to the velvety sound of his voice.

"There she is!"

She paused. Her brain, still recovering from its shock, was slow to process Mason standing in front of her, his arms outstretched.

He shot a look at the officer before closing the gap between them and wrapping her in a hug. "How are you, honey? Are you okay?"

She nodded. "Yeah."

"Thank you, officer," Mason said, waving with one hand. He put an arm around Lillian and led her out the front door.

She walked along with him, her chest heavy, her breathing picking up once more.

Once they were outside, he stopped and faced her, putting both hands on her shoulders. "No really, are you okay?"

"I don't know."

"What happened?"

Lillian opened her mouth and nothing but a whimper escaped.

Mason pulled her in. His arms were warm, and only then did she realize how cold she'd gotten. She nestled her face into his chest. He smelled like he always had, the same old cologne she'd bought him for Christmas year after year.

"Only family was allowed to visit, so I had to tell them I was your husband. Sorry."

It had been ages since she'd been hugged like this. It was... nice. She closed her eyes.

"I hadn't heard from you in so long and I was worried," he said. "I called Lucy and she told me you'd been arrested."

Ah, of course. Everyone would know soon. "Yeah."

He pulled back, looking her in the eyes. "*What* were you doing?"

"We had a gift basket, and we wanted to drop it off in Gunther's room."

"Okay."

She dropped her voice. "But Lucy wanted me to look around, because she thinks...I don't know, she thinks Gunther is up to something, and so I did, and this woman found me and called the police."

He frowned, touching a hand to her cheek. "We'll figure it out. I don't know Gunther that well, but I'll talk to him. See what I can do."

"He must be so angry," she said. "He's going to sue the hotel."

Mason laughed. "He's not going to sue the hotel. It'll be fine. I promise."

In that moment, their differences seemed quite small. She remembered why she'd loved him all these years, why they tried to make it work again and again. He could be a bit much, but in his own way, he did love her.

"Lillian!"

She spun, spotting Chief Hank getting out of his truck. Lucy must have called Margie.

Lillian took a step away from Mason. "Hey, Chief."

He reached them quickly. "What's going on?"

"I got myself into some trouble. It's not –"

Mason cut her off. "Oh no, nah nah nah. We're not talking to any cops without our lawyer present."

Lillian clenched her jaw. "Mason, it's fine. Chief Hank is a friend of my mom's."

Hank cracked a smile. "This guy's about to read me the riot act."

"Don't fall for it," Mason said, taking Lillian by the hand and trying to lead her off. "We should go."

"It's fine." She pulled away. The muscles in her neck and jaw were stiff. "Really."

Hank barely looked at Mason before addressing Lillian again. "Listen, kid. It sounds like the guy who was staying in the room – Garrett?"

"Gunther," she corrected.

"Yeah. He wants to press charges. Says you had no business being in his room."

Her chest tightened. It was as bad as she'd imagined. Maybe worse.

"It'll be fine," Mason said. "This is stupid. This whole thing is a farce."

Hank flinched ever so slightly, as though Mason was nothing more than a fly buzzing near his ear, then went on. "Lucy called and threatened to sue me if I didn't help you."

Lillian let out a weak laugh. "That's nice of her."

"Yeah." He chuckled. "It'll be all right. These tangles happen sometimes. You didn't steal anything, did you?"

"No!"

"Good." He let out a sigh and smiled. "All right, good. Do you need a ride back to Orcas?"

"She has a ride." Mason cut off her reply. "I borrowed Aaron's yacht."

As much as she didn't want to go near Aaron's weird yacht, she didn't want to put Chief Hank out. He had a job to do and didn't need to waste his time chauffeuring criminals like her around. "I guess I'm taking the yacht."

"Keep your nose clean, kid. I'll be in touch." Hank nodded to her, looked at Mason, and turned to walk into the jail.

"You didn't have to answer him, you know," Mason said in a low voice. "He's just trying to get you to admit you're guilty."

"No, he isn't. He's a friend."

"Don't be so naive, Lillian." He stared at her for a moment, then let out a sigh. "Why did you get yourself into this?"

She searched her mind. What was it? Was she that easily persuaded by pancakes?

That wasn't it. The pancakes were an excuse. She'd told Lucy "no" to dozens of schemes over the years.

This time was different. She had been worried about Dustin, worried enough to do something utterly reckless.

She couldn't tell Mason this, of course. She couldn't tell anyone.

So she shrugged.

Mason stared at her, narrowing his eyes and pursing his lips. "You've not been yourself recently."

"You think?" Lillian let out a laugh. That was the understatement of the year.

"Love can make you do crazy things."

A breath caught in her throat.

How did he know? How could he know she had so desperately believed Dustin was in trouble and needed her help, that she had hoped it was Dustin who had come to her rescue, the one who plagued her thoughts day and night?

He smiled down at her and grabbed both of her hands. "I know. I've been half crazy missing you, too."

Oh, no. She pulled her hands away. "Mason. I appreciate you coming here, but –"

He cracked a smile, pushing his sunglasses over his eyes. "Yeah, yeah, I know. I'll give you your space." He jerked his head toward the water. "Luxury awaits. You ready? Do you have all your stuff?"

She cast one look back at the jail. No one else was coming for her, and she felt so tired. "Yeah."

Chapter Twenty

"The San Juan Islands are home to the largest breeding population of bald eagles in the lower forty-eight states." Dustin paused, then pointed up. "Did you hear that? That's the call of one now!"

"Cut!" Gunther yelled, rushing over and putting a hand on Dustin's shoulder. "That was perfect. We'll add an eagle cry in post-production, then cut to the footage of an eagle in a tree."

He looked up into the trees. They were shooting in the state park along one of the many hiking trails. Unfortunately, they hadn't found any eagles.

Dustin had known that would be the case after talking to one of the naturalists who worked on San Juan Island, but Gunther still wanted the shot in the woods. And so, they'd spent the day shooting footage of Dustin walking up and down the trail. They'd seen a short-eared owl, an American Kestrel, and even a quail with beautifully speckled white-and-black plumage on his neck, but not a single eagle.

He turned back to Gunther. "You've heard a bald eagle cry before, right?"

"Of course I have. It's a crazy powerful scream. We should put it in the intro. Make it a little more patriotic."

He winced. They should've talked about this. Dustin was finding a lot of things they should've talked about. "The call is weaker than you'd expect. They kind of peep, almost like a seagull, but softer."

"No way, man, I've heard eagles before."

"Yeah...if you heard it on TV, they're usually using a red-tailed hawk's call. That's the scream you know."

Gunther covered his eyes with his hand. "You're telling me this now?"

Ariel, who had been caught in conversation with the cameraman, jogged over. "Everything okay?"

Gunther turned to her. "Did you know about the eagles?"

"What eagles?"

He sighed, and Dustin inserted himself back into the conversation. "I think it'd be interesting if we told the audience how bald eagles actually sound. I'm sure most of them won't know, and people like to get little snippets of information like that. Trivia."

Gunther weighed this for a moment before uncrossing his arms. "Fine. Okay, yeah. I guess that could be good. I need to make some calls."

He walked down the trail, disappearing around a bend into the trees.

Ariel stood with her hands on her hips. She let out a breath, her cheeks puffing out.

"What's going on with him?" Dustin asked.

She scrunched her nose. "He's mad at me."

"Ah. Is this still because of the foxes? He'll get over it."

The week prior, Ariel had mistakenly sent Dustin and the rest of the crew looking for foxes all over Orcas Island. They had gone to Turtleback Mountain, then Coho Preserve near Olga, and finally Moran State Park.

They had wasted two days searching before Dustin had looked into it and realized the elusive red foxes lived on San Juan Island, not on Orcas Island. Unlike the black-tailed deer, they did not take swimming trips between the islands.

He felt bad about that one. It was his mistake, assuming Ariel knew where the foxes were. He should have questioned it, just as Ariel should have questioned that Gunther knew what he was talking about when he'd announced "It's fox week!"

Ultimately, it was Gunther who had changed their shooting schedule that week and, not realizing they needed to travel to San Juan, he was the one who wasted everyone's time.

He was the boss, though, and shifted the blame to Ariel. It was a domino effect of miscommunication and rushing, and the resulting frosty attitudes were becoming the new norm.

"Don't remind me," she said, shaking her head. "No, this was something else."

"What happened? Maybe I can help."

Ariel looked up, fidgeting with her hands. "I doubt it. Just tell Lillian I'm sorry."

"Dustin," the director called out, "let's try the eagle thing again. The lighting wasn't great and your face looked weird."

"Hang on a minute," he said, shooting a glance at him before turning back to Ariel. "What does Lillian have to do with this?"

"You didn't hear?" She frowned. "I assumed you were close...well, I guess if she's still being processed, she might not have –"

"Being processed?"

Ariel grimaced, her lips twisting as she looked away. "She was arrested, Dustin. I'm sorry. I thought you knew."

It felt like his lungs had deflated. He had to remind himself to breathe. "For what?"

Ariel got closer and dropped her voice. "She asked if she could leave a gift basket for Gunther in his room, and I said sure. I didn't think he'd care, you know? But then Anette, one of the production assistants, saw her in his room and called the cops, and...I don't know. Gunther is so angry with me."

"That's ridiculous. I'll talk to him."

"No! Just let it go. It's fine. We always make up in the end."

It wasn't Ariel Dustin was worried about. Not that he was going to tell her that.

The director called out again. "Dustin!"

"You'd better go," Ariel said with a nod. "They need you."

"They can wait." He waved a hand over his head and called out. "I'll be back in ten."

Dustin didn't wait for a response. He went off in search of Gunther, walking down the winding trail back to the parking lot. Gunther's car was gone.

Great.

Dustin pulled out his phone. No signal.

Terrific.

He looked back toward the trail. There were still a few hours of daylight. The crew could wait. Maybe an eagle would land on their heads while he was away.

He got into his car and drove.

The drive out of the park was a slow one, and he had to be careful around bikers and hikers. He decided to make some calls as he drove. The first was to Lillian.

Unfortunately, she didn't answer, so he tried Lucy.

She picked up after two rings. "Took you long enough!"

"I just found out what happened. Where's Lillian? Is she okay?"

"She was bailed out and she's on her way back to the island." Lucy paused. "What do you know?"

He slowed to navigate around a pair of bikers. "Ariel said she gave Lillian permission to drop off a gift basket, Lillian got arrested for it, and Gunther is mad at her."

"Mad at Lillian?"

"No, mad at Ariel. I guess at Lillian, too? I don't understand. I'm going to talk to him."

"Erm. Yeah, go talk to him. Tell him to stop being a pain in my neck."

"Is there anything else I need to know?"

The line went silent.

"Lucy, you still there?"

"Yeah! Still here. Go talk to Gunther. Threaten him, maybe."

At the exit of the park, he saw Gunther's car pulled over on the side of the road. "All right, just found him. Talk to you later."

He hung up, carefully parked his car behind Gunther's, and got out. Dustin slowly approached Gunther's driver's side door and knocked on the window.

Gunther jumped, looking at him with wide eyes.

"Sorry," he mouthed.

Gunther gave him a "wait" finger, ended his call and rolled down the window. "What's up?"

He should've planned what he was going to say. He couldn't exactly accuse his boss of being a pain in the neck, as Lucy had suggested. "I need to talk to you."

"Right now?"

"Yeah." He paused. Time to think fast. "Your and Ariel's relationship – it's not healthy. It's bringing down the crew."

Gunther groaned, running a hand through his hair. "She's a bad communicator, Dustin."

As though he were any better. Pointing fingers wasn't going to help now, though. "I know."

"We chased those foxes for days."

Dustin laughed. "Yeah, but that was a miscommunication on *all* ends, don't you think?"

"Yeah, sure. I'll talk to her." He rolled his eyes. "Anything else?"

Dustin cleared his throat. "What about this stuff with the gift basket?"

"What about it?"

"Ariel told Lillian she could drop it off. I don't think she deserved to be arrested and –"

Gunther interrupted him. "I don't have time for this right now, Dustin. We're falling behind, our funding is up in the air, and Ariel can't tell anyone what they're supposed to be doing. Can't it wait?"

"Fine." He put his hands up. "We can talk about it later."

Gunther was already rolling the window back up and waving him off. "Good. See ya."

He made the walk back to his car. Lillian had been on his mind for weeks, and now she was bursting through. He thought avoiding her would help, but it seemed to only worsen the problem.

Enough was enough. It didn't matter why he was like this, it didn't matter why he couldn't stop thinking about her. Dustin was sick of fighting it.

Just because he didn't believe in love, it didn't mean he didn't care about her. She needed his help. That was all that mattered. He wasn't a monster, and the image of her sitting in a jail cell made his stomach turn. It wasn't like he would accidentally stumble into proposing to her again if he spent some time with her.

Probably.

"I can still care about her without being in love with her," he muttered to himself as he started the car.

Chapter Twenty-one

Maybe it had been a mistake to take Mason's call, but Lucy was desperate. She had already called Marty, her boss Fiona at the farm, Chip, Chief Hank, and Margie. No one else was able to get Lillian out of jail so quickly. Mason happened to be in the right place at the right time, and he had access to a boat.

She'd tried to avoid tipping off Claire, but it didn't work. Chip had blabbed everything to her.

Yet, surprisingly, when Claire had called Lucy, she wasn't angry, even after Lucy admitted their scheme. Though Claire thought they shouldn't have gone into Gunther's room, she also believed Gunther was being "silly," and said if he couldn't get over himself, she was going to "kick him and all of his friends out of the hotel."

Lucy asked her to hold off on that for the time being. She ended the call and paced the apartment, cleaning as she went. There were papers to tidy, cabinets to wipe, and baseboards to dust. It kept her hands busy and her mind from spiraling.

When she heard a knock at the door, she sprinted over, opening it to find Rob.

"I thought you were leaving for Seattle!" She threw her arms around him, squeezing him tight.

"How can I leave when your crime ring is just starting to take off?"

Lucy released him and stepped back, hanging her head. "It's fallen apart more spectacularly than I'd imagined."

"It'll be all right," he said, stepping into the apartment. "Is Lillian back yet?"

"No. I never should've trusted Mason." She peered around the corner. There was no sign of either of them. "He's probably forcing her to sit through a candlelit dinner right now."

Rob laughed. "I doubt it. What did Dustin say?"

"That he'd talk to Gunther." She let out a groan. "Why did you let me get carried away with my Gunther theory?"

"As if I could stop you."

She shook her head. "I know. You're so weak when it comes to standing up to me."

"Hey!"

"What?" She put her hands on her hips. "What good is a boyfriend if I can't blame him for my failures?"

Rob frowned. "Fair enough. I'll allow it."

A call from Marty popped onto her phone and she answered right away. He said he hadn't found any dirt on Gunther, but that he'd keep looking.

When Lucy got off the phone, Rob shot her a look. "I thought you were upset that your conspiring got everyone into trouble. Why are you pulling Marty into it now?"

"He's a computer wizard. He could probably hack Gunther's laptop if we needed it."

It seemed like Rob was about to launch into scolding her when the door to the apartment opened. Lucy sucked in a breath and held it.

Lillian walked in with a weak, "Hi," and Mason trailed behind.

Lucy was ready to accept her punishment. "Lil, I am so sorry. This is all my fault."

Lillian looked at her, then at Rob, before sitting on the couch. "It's not your fault."

Mason ignored this interaction and instead nodded at Rob. "Hey, I'm Mason. I don't think we've met."

Rob shook his head, a grin on his face. "No, but I've heard a lot about you."

Lucy turned slowly, shooting a glare at him. He thought this was *funny*! "Maybe it's time for you to go, Rob."

"Oh, you're Rob!" Mason let out a sigh. "I was afraid you were Lillian's new boyfriend or something."

"That's the other Rob," he quipped, and Lucy smacked him in the arm.

Mason stared at him for a moment. "Ha. Right."

He seemed unsure if Rob was joking, but Lucy didn't care. Her focus was on Lillian. "Were they mean to you?"

She'd pulled a pillow onto her lap. "No."

"Were you scared?"

Lillian shrugged, staring at her hands.

Lucy took a seat next to her. "I am so, so sorry. Please just yell at me. Just get it over with."

"I'm not going to yell at you, Lucy." She looked up. The whites of her eyes were red, and her mouth was firmly down-turned. "I have no one to blame but myself."

"You fell into bad habits," Mason offered. "It's not totally your fault."

Lucy had forgotten how much she disliked Mason. If only her ploy to bring Dustin back into Lillian's life had worked.

She had sent him their address, so where was he? He should have been here to swoop Lillian off her feet hours ago. "Lillian doesn't have bad habits."

"She does when it comes to getting into trouble with you," Mason said, matter-of-factly. "Seems to be a common thing out here."

"She's better off here than locked away, waiting for you in a tower," Lucy shot back.

"Is it? Because thanks to you, I just had to bail her out of jail."

Lucy stood and took a step toward him. "Thanks to *you*, she wasted seven years of her –"

"Guys!" Lillian got out of her seat. "Please. I just want to take a nap."

"Yeah, give her a break." Mason put a hand on her shoulder. "You look tired. Do you think you're getting sick?" He made a face. "I can't afford to get sick right now."

If only Lucy had gotten Mason arrested instead. That would've solved all her problems.

"I don't think so." Lillian rubbed her face with her hand. "I just need some sleep."

Another knock at the door. They fell silent.

"Do you think it's the police again?" Lillian asked, wide-eyed.

"No, of course not," Lucy lied, crossing the apartment. That was exactly what they didn't need to happen. Maybe they were coming to take Lucy as a conspirator?

That was fine with her. Better her than Lillian. She took a breath before opening the door. "Oh! Hi!"

Dustin looked older, somehow, his face creased with lines. "Hey. Have you heard from Lillian?"

She stepped aside, waving an arm behind her. "She just got home."

Mason grinned. "Dusty, Dusty, Dustin. Are you here to get dirt for Gunther?"

Dustin barely glanced at him. "I'm here for Lillian."

"What?" Mason made a face. "I don't buy it. Trust no one, Lil."

Lillian was supposed to trust no one but Mason? What a weirdly controlling thing to say.

"They go *way* back," Lucy said, unable to contain her sneer.

Another sign that Mason had never listened to Lillian speak. How could he not know who her *only* ex was? It wasn't like there were a ton to keep track of.

Lucy knew every one of Rob's ex-girlfriends. She was an encyclopedia of them, with a working knowledge of their likes, hobbies, nicknames, where they had shopped, and how and why their relationship with Rob hadn't worked out.

It was important information. It was Rob's love history – it was partially why he was who he was today! How could Mason just not care to know any of that about Lillian?

"I'm sorry about all of this, Dustin," Lillian said. "I didn't mean to get you in trouble."

"I'm not in trouble." Dustin hesitated, then leaned in to give her a quick hug. "Are you in trouble?"

"I think so."

Mason was typing away on his phone and spoke without looking up. "How about you go lie down, Lillian? I need to meet with Aaron now, but I'll talk to Gunther later. Or I'll get Aaron to talk to Gunther. That might work."

Lillian's eyes lingered on Dustin for a moment. "Okay."

Mason missed it entirely. He slipped his phone into his pocket and flashed a smile at her.

As much as she wanted to get back to slinging insults, Lucy wasn't going to waste an opportunity to get rid of him. She walked to the door and opened it. "Well, if you need to run, then take care, Mason."

He sauntered over, winking at her as he walked through the door. "Stay out of trouble, Lucy."

Lucy locked the door behind him and returned to the group in the living room.

"I tried talking to Gunther," Dustin said, "but he's got some weird grudge going on with Ariel right now. She told me herself, though, that she gave you permission to drop off the basket, so he has to get over it, right?"

"Oh, is that all this is about?" Lucy could kiss him. "That's not a big deal, then, is it, Lil?"

Lillian's smile faded and she took a seat. "I was caught in the act, Lucy."

"What act? There was no act." She forced a smile at Dustin, then turned back to Lillian, the smile frozen on her face. "We just wanted to be nice."

"It's okay, Lucy. You don't have to lie for me."

"It's not a lie," she insisted. "We are *incredibly* nice."

Lillian let out a sigh. "Dustin, you probably shouldn't be associated with us."

"Why?" He took a seat in a side chair, his gaze never leaving her.

Lucy shot a look at Rob. Was he seeing this? Was he seeing this absolute devotion on Dustin's face?

Rob caught her gaze and raised his eyebrows.

Okay, no, he wasn't seeing it. She'd have to explain it to him later.

Lillian spoke again. "We weren't just dropping off a gift basket."

"We were fostering friendships," Lucy interrupted, her voice a little too loud.

"Lucy." Lillian's voice was soft, but firm. "I'm not going to cover this up."

She sat back in her seat. "Fine."

Lillian paused for a moment before spilling the beans, one by one, to Dustin. She told him about Gunther's failed business, Lucy's subsequent suspicions, and the plan she and Lucy had hatched.

Even Lucy had to admit that, when stated out loud, the plan sounded pretty silly.

"When I got in the room, it felt all wrong," she said. "I was going to drop the basket and leave. But then I saw Lucy's picture."

Lucy sat up. "Excuse me, what?"

She nodded, telling them about a folder filled with newspaper articles, pictures, and a random scientist's business card.

"Hang on," Lucy said. "Either Gunther is onto me, or I'm one hundred percent right that he's up to something shady."

"It sounds like he was doing research about the community," Dustin said. "Maybe he looked you up because you were his contact for the hotel?"

That was far too rational, and further, it didn't feel right. Lucy shook her head. "Or maybe he looked me up because he knows I would figure out his scheme."

"She is great with schemes," Rob said with a sigh. "If anyone can figure out what Gunther is up to, it's Lucy."

"I don't think he's some evil mastermind," Dustin said.

"Then why is he so mad that Lillian found this folder?" asked Lucy.

"He isn't. He's mad at Ariel and getting back at her through Lillian."

"Could be both," Rob offered. "He did leave a trail of customers covered in boils."

Lucy and Lillian both winced. The pictures in the lawsuit were jarring enough to haunt Lucy's dreams.

"To be honest," Dustin said with a frown, "I'm not shocked to hear Gunther has a history like that."

Lucy leaned forward. "So you admit it. He's shady."

"Not shady." He paused, searching for the words. "He has a lot of ideas, but not always the best execution. We actually have that in common."

"How many bankrupted companies have you left behind?" Rob asked.

Dustin let out a laugh. "None so far. This will be my first."

"Don't say that." Lillian was sitting up straight, looking much more awake.

Maybe she wasn't so tired after all. Maybe Mason had just been sucking the life out of her.

"We'll see. Gunther isn't making it easy on anyone. Maybe that's how all shows are." Dustin shrugged, his stare still fixed on Lillian. "I'm going out on the boat tomorrow, just me and the cameraman, to shoot some promos while Gunther is out of town. Would you want to come?"

Lillian bit her lip. "What if he finds out I was there and gets mad?"

"Then I'll tell him to stop being a brat or I'll quit," Dustin said.

Lillian laughed, a real, hearty laugh. "I don't think that'll help your career."

"Who needs a career?" He waved a hand. "We might see whales. I mean, probably not, because they've been avoiding us, but maybe."

Lucy was about to say something, but Rob caught her eye and gave her a stern look.

She smiled to herself. So he *had* noticed the love affair blossoming in front of him, and he wanted her to stay out of it.

Fine.

"Are you sure Gunther won't be there?" Lillian asked.

"One hundred percent. He just left the island." Dustin leaned toward her, a smile dancing on his face. "If he shows up and causes trouble, we'll Gilligan him."

"Gilligan him?" Lillian cocked her head to the side. "What does that mean?"

"Leave him on one of the remote islands." He laughed. "The producers were joking about it today. Aren't there some islands that are state parks? Islands without ferry service?"

Lucy couldn't stand being out of the conversation any longer. "Yeah, like James Island."

"That's one. We'll leave him there." He grinned at her. "What do you say?"

Lucy had to grit her teeth to keep quiet.

Say yes, say yes, you fool!

"If you think it'll be okay."

"It'll be great."

Lucy clapped her hands together. "Great! Just what Lillian needs. Who wants pizza?"

Chapter Twenty-two

The hat and sunglasses disguise Lillian had put together for the boat ride proved to be unnecessary. As promised, the only people on the boat were Dustin, the captain, and the cameraman, Percy.

"You did manage to trick Percy into thinking you're a celebrity with those huge sunglasses," Dustin said as they floated away from the dock. "So there's that."

They were standing near the bow of the ship, shoulder to shoulder, hands leaning over the railing. It was a stunning day, the sky a rich blue with enough clouds to keep the sun from being a bother. The water was calm, and the whale-watching boat sliced through the surface smoothly.

She pulled the brim of her baseball cap down and peered up at him. "Do you think he'll tell Gunther I'm here?"

"I think he'd throw Gunther into the harbor if he knew you went to jail over a gift basket."

"It wasn't just a gift basket," she said, voice low. "You know that."

He bumped into her with his hip. "I know. Your heart was in the right place, though. It always is."

Lillian looked out onto the water, unable to stop herself from grinning.

Maybe there was something to it. After Dustin had left their apartment the day before, Lucy babbled for over an hour about how lovingly Dustin had looked at her, how obvious it was that he still cared, and insisted he was "seconds away from proposing again."

That was a bit much, and Lillian refused to even consider it. She would have dismissed the entire argument were it not for the off-handed comment Rob had made. "He misses you," he said. "Whatever it's worth, I can tell he does."

The idea stuck in her head, along with the solemn way Dustin had said "I'm here for Lillian" when he arrived at the apartment.

Presumably, Mason had been there for the same reason, but it had felt different. He was texting on his phone, cracking jokes, trying to fight with Lucy.

She couldn't help but wonder – was it Mason who wanted her back, or Dustin?

It was too much to hope for. For now, she wanted to focus on enjoying the moment.

The boat glided on, passing a patch of rocks that jutted from the water. There were a few harbor seals laid out in the sun and a flock of stocky birds calling out with a chorus of jeers. They were robin-sized, with long beaks, charcoal feathers, and puffy white bellies.

"What kind of birds are those?" she asked.

"Black Turnstones," he said. "If we were closer, you could see them flipping rocks. They'll eat the bugs they find underneath. They also eat mollusks, barnacles, even berries."

"They're so fat and cute." She let out a laugh. "You should put that in the show. A fat, cute bird episode."

"It would be a hit."

A voice shouted from behind them. "Hey, good news!"

Lillian jumped. She hadn't heard Percy sneak up.

Dustin turned. "What's up?"

"Some transient orcas were spotted coming up Haro Strait. The captain's going to swing us around San Juan to see if we can catch a glimpse."

He looked at Lillian, a grin on his face. "I've been dying to see orcas since we got here."

Percy nodded. According to Dustin, he was the only cameraman on the crew with experience shooting in nature. The rest were all commercial guys and, apparently, they were struggling.

Percy also had the least tolerance for Gunther's whimsies. "Do you still want to get some promo clips on the way there?"

Dustin nodded, then looked to Lillian. "You don't mind, do you?"

"No, of course not." She stepped back, finding her way to a bench on the side of the boat.

She watched as Dustin and Percy debated positioning before starting to roll.

"Come along as we venture into the rugged beauty of the islands and uncover hidden gems of the Salish Sea."

Dustin paused for a moment, then jumped to, "All of this and more as we dive into an island paradise and uncover the hidden wonders of the natural world."

After ten minutes of similar introductions, he threw in a, "We're going to have a *whale* of a good time!"

Dustin and Lillian cracked up at that one, but Percy was all business. "Playful is fine, but try to be less cheesy."

He thought on this for a moment, then nodded. "Welcome to the San Juan Islands, an enchanted archipelago tucked away in the corner of the country. Together we'll explore secret coves, rare wildlife, and..." he trailed off, flashing a look at Lillian. "Hang on, I need to think."

She was probably making him feel self-conscious. Lillian stood from her seat and walked to the back of the boat. It was less windy there, and the noise from the engine canceled out other sounds. The hum was calming, in a way, and she gazed out onto the water and the passing islands, feeling like she was in a trance.

She hadn't heard anything more about her arrest. It was possible Gunther would cool off, or that Dustin would be able to get through to him. It seemed Aaron could have some sway, too. Gunther certainly liked sucking up to him. Come to think of it, so did Mason.

She hadn't heard from Mason since yesterday and dreaded him resuming his pushiness. Lillian needed to make it clear that while she was thankful he'd stepped in and helped her, they were not getting back together. It was awkward and painful on all sides, but it was for the best. Especially if Dustin still had even a whisper of how he'd once felt...

The engine abruptly cut out and the boat slowed to a stop, bobbing in the water.

She walked to the front of the boat. "Is everything okay?"

"We might have some whales swimming by in about half an hour," Dustin said, eyes bright. "We're just going to sit here and wait."

"Oh. Cool!" She watched as Percy walked down the side of the boat, filming the island shore in the distance. "Is it okay if I hang out up here again?"

"Yeah. Sorry if I was boring you."

"I wasn't bored. I didn't want to cramp your style."

"Me?" He shot her a sideways glance. "Never."

She was about to tease him when he pulled his phone from his pocket.

"Sorry," he said, "one second." He cleared his throat and answered a call. "Hello?" A pause. "We're waiting on whales. Just me, the captain, Percy, and Lillian."

Lillian tried to pretend like she wasn't eavesdropping, but she couldn't help it. She was standing so close she could clearly hear Ariel say, "If Gunther knew Lillian were there, he'd tell you to throw her into the ocean."

Dustin's response was swift. "Tell Gunther if he messes with her, I'll throw *him* in the ocean. I'm not joking. I have to go."

He ended the call, shoving the phone back into his pocket.

They stood there, listening to the waves hitting the hull of the boat. Lillian decided it was silly to pretend like she hadn't heard. "So...it seems like he's still mad."

Dustin's eyes flitted to her, then back onto the water. "Yeah. I'm sorry."

"It's not your fault. Not at all. I don't know why you're being so nice to me."

He turned to face her. "Don't you?"

The full focus of his gaze made her heart leap. There was no air in her lungs, and her voice came out small and weak. "I don't."

"You're –" He broke eye contact, looking over her head for a moment. "We're friends. We go way back, like Lucy said."

Friends.

The word had never felt so heavy, or so dry.

"Yeah." She forced a smile. "Way back."

Chapter Twenty-three

What a fumble. He'd completely chickened out. Was he really going to admit, out loud, that there was no one like her, and he was being nice to her because he'd never stopped loving her?

They were just feelings. Love. Longing. It didn't mean anything. It wasn't possible to stop loving someone. It didn't mean they could ever make it work, and it didn't mean he had to force his feelings on her. He'd be no better than Mason, begging her for a second chance.

A look of confusion – or was it hurt? – had crossed her face so briefly when he said they were friends. It was a flash, then she had looked out onto the sea and asked which direction the whales might come from.

Still. Being friends was better than the devastation he'd gotten out of his last relationship.

Maybe she needed to know about that. Maybe she'd want to know, even.

"My brother's getting married in December," he announced.

She turned to face him. Her expression was recovered, a polite smile on her face. "Oh? I didn't know he was engaged. How's he been?"

"Good. He's been good."

"Do you like his fiancée?"

He laughed, running his hand along the railing. "I do. So much so that I wanted to marry her myself."

She raised her eyebrows. "What?"

"His fiancée was…" A cough escaped him. He'd spent too much time talking promos, and his throat was dry. He'd keep it short. "She used to be my fiancée."

Lillian's mouth popped open, and she gaped at him for a moment before shaking it off. "What happened?"

"We'd been dating for a few months, I proposed – you know, as is my habit."

She smiled.

He went on. "Two months before the wedding, they sat me down and told me they'd fallen in love."

"Dustin." She shook her head. "That's awful."

"They asked for my blessing, which, you know…I didn't want her to be unhappy. I didn't want either of them to be unhappy."

For a moment, she said nothing, watching him with those big, soulful eyes. Finally, she spoke, her voice soft. "What about you, Dustin? What about you? Weren't you angry?"

Angry. Hurt. Betrayed and, not to mention, blindsided. Yet everyone in his family, including his parents, treated the whole thing as if it were some happy accident that she'd met Dustin first.

"The heart desires what the heart desires," he finally said.

The water rippled, and he pointed with a shout. "Orcas?"

The captain popped his head out of the cabin. "You'd know if it was an orca. Probably just a porpoise."

"Ah." He turned back to her. "That's how it goes, I guess."

"That's absurd." The wind blew her hair in front of her eyes and she pushed it away. "Your brother has always been selfish."

"I guess so," he said with a shrug.

"I'm not just saying that because he never liked me."

He turned to her, unable to keep the smile off his face. "What?"

Lillian smiled back at him. "Come on, you think I didn't know?"

"He liked you. I mean – I'm sure he still likes you."

"Not enough to try to marry me," she said wistfully.

A laugh burst out of him. "No, apparently not."

"Mason kept telling me he was going to propose," she said, staring out onto the horizon. "He never did."

Whoa, what?

Dustin dropped his gaze. Was that all their fighting was? Was that why they had broken up? Mason had dragged his feet to get engaged, and she broke things off?

It seemed like Mason had gotten the message. He'd come to her rescue at the jail. Maybe now he'd propose and they could live happily ever after.

Dustin could hardly keep the disappointment off his face. All this time he'd been worried about something happening between them. He tried to fight it, then avoid it, and now –

now he knew. It was all for nothing. She was still in love with Mason. Of course she was.

"Oh," he finally said, then immediately changed the topic. "Are you hungry? We've got some stuff in the cooler."

"Uh, yeah. Sure."

He left her to fetch the food, and the topic of engagements didn't resurface for the rest of the trip.

The orcas never made their appearance, so after a few hours they gave up. When they were back on dry land, he thought about inviting her out to that dinner, but decided not to at the last minute. She had enough going on, and probably had plans with Mason.

Instead, he went back to his hotel room and worked through the emails that had piled up during the day. There was still no sign of Gunther, but Ariel had sent them all a tentative schedule for the coming week, and he was expected to return tomorrow.

It was smart for Ariel to get it in writing. It would help avoid the confusion they'd been suffering through recently. Then again, it might not. Gunther didn't like schedules, claiming they stifled his creativity.

Dustin had looked into Lucy's findings about Gunther's last company, and, knowing Gunther, it was easy to see why it had failed. A company like that wasn't the right fit for him. The show was much better. There were more people involved, people who had more experience and who could keep righting the ship whenever his whims threw them off course.

Or at least, Dustin hoped that was the case. His old position at the vet clinic had been filled. There was no going back.

He missed doing videos for his channel, though. Hopefully he could get back to making some videos soon; a few fans had emailed asking what was going on.

Dustin still found it hard to believe he had fans. Maybe he could record something short, a check-in, something fun. There were a lot of kids who watched his channel; surely they'd like to see a starfish, or a whale, if he was ever lucky enough to come across one.

He logged into the email for the account and one message caught his eye immediately. The subject line said, "I thought you should know."

He opened it and began reading.

Dear Dustin,

My twelve-year-old son Joey and I were huge fans of your channel. We loved watching the episodes together and learning about different animals. For a while, it was the only thing he wanted to talk about. He wanted to be just like you.

That all changed a few weeks ago. Joey recently stopped talking about becoming a veterinarian. I couldn't figure out what had happened, but then I went on your Instagram. You were tagged in a picture with Mason Fink.

Mason is Joey's father.

I had Joey when I was a senior in high school. The things his family said about me are not worth repeating. None of them have ever met Joey. They never wanted to, and we didn't need them.

I gave Joey the option to reach out to his dad when he was ten. Mason never responded to his emails, or to his calls.

I can't express how deeply this affected him. Maybe you can imagine. Maybe you can't, but I think seeing you, his idol, with the father who never wanted him broke his heart all over again.

You may like Mason, and maybe he's helping you with your new show. But I wanted you to know Joey and I will not be watching it.

Sincerely,

Kara

It was a punch to the gut. His hands went cold, and he reread the email.

Then he hit reply and started typing a response.

Dear Joey and Kara,

Please believe me when I say I had no idea about Mason.

He stopped and stared at the screen as a thought dawned on him. He'd had no idea about Mason. That was believable – he had just met the guy, and he didn't like him anyway.

But that begged the question – what did Lillian know?

Chapter Twenty-four

In spite of her troubles, Lillian's life went on. The day of her mom's wedding shower arrived, and as she stood in the ballroom of The Grand Madrona Hotel, she decided it was time to be thankful.

Margie had managed to pull together a remarkably beautiful event. Twinkling lights lined the towering windows of the ballroom, and each of the twenty tables was draped in white linen and topped with pink flowers.

At the far side of the room, a table overflowed with beautifully wrapped gifts, all elegant bows and ribbon. Next to it was the dessert table, with cookies and pastries piled high and a pyramid of cupcakes in the center.

A string quartet was just setting up as Lillian walked in. She'd asked Margie about it and got a breathless response. "They played at a wedding at the barn recently. They do 90's hits in a classical style. Isn't that darling? I thought Claire would just *love* it. I had to hire them!"

The ballroom was filled with family and friends. Margie had sent out the invitations, and Lucy had followed up with every guest to make sure they had a way to get to the island and a place to stay. Lillian felt guilty she hadn't been more involved, but it seemed her help wasn't needed. Lucy and Margie were a force to be reckoned with.

It was meant to be a joint wedding shower for both the bride and groom. They didn't have much family to speak of – Marty and his girlfriend Emma were there, of course, as well as Aunt Becca, but the rest of their guests were friends. Chip had a lot of family, including distant cousins he'd recently reconnected with through his trips to the Lummi reservation in Bellingham.

Between all the hugs and joking around, Lillian didn't have time to feel sorry for herself. She was thankful for the joy that filled the room, and most of all, she was thrilled for her mom and Chip. They looked so happy, and they were surrounded by love.

The merriment was so engrossing that Lillian entirely missed Mason sneaking into the ballroom.

At that moment, Aunt Becca was regaling her with a story about a fire drill they'd had in elementary school. "Me and Claire got so scared that it was real, we ran all the way home!"

Lillian covered her face, laughing and imagining her mom running away from school. Her eyes were closed when she felt two hands slither around her waist from behind.

"There's my girl," Mason said.

Lillian jumped, snapping her head back to see who it was. When she caught Mason's grin, she had the urge to push him away.

There were a hundred things she wanted to say. She wanted to thank him for his help but tell him it was over. They were not getting back together. Stop contacting her, stop calling, stop showing up!

To her shame, however, she couldn't think of any of that in the moment. Instead she froze, turning into a statue.

"I'm loving this cello version of Barbie Girl," he added, resting his chin on her shoulder. "Who knew it was always meant to be a classical piece?"

Becca, eyes darting between them, stopped talking and excused herself with a smile. Lillian was left to fend for herself.

"Mason," she finally managed to say.

He spun to face her, latching onto her hands. "Maybe we'll have a party just like this for our engagement."

She tried to pull her hands away, but he had tightened his grip.

"Please," he said, "don't be like that."

"Be like what?" She lowered her voice. They didn't need to make a scene. "We're not together anymore."

"But we could be." His eyes were wide and pleading. "I haven't gotten to talk to you, Lil. I've changed. I've really thought about what you said."

"Mason..." Her voice trailed off. It was not in her nature to be cruel, and as annoying as he could be, she still didn't want to hurt him.

"You were right about everything. You were right about my job. I know I work too much. But now – since you've been gone – I'm just thinking and thinking. All of my friends are off getting married, and what do I have?" He paused. "Nothing. It's all worth nothing without you."

"I don't want to talk about this right now."

Undeterred, he pressed on. "You know what I realized? I'm going to have a million dollars one day and no one to share it with."

"A million dollars!" Lucy stepped in, a glass of champagne in hand. "Deary me, that's a lot of dollars."

His face stiffened into a smile. "Hi, Lucy."

She rested the glass against her cheek. "Lil, Rose just got to the island. Marty is going to go and pick her up from the ferry."

"I'll go too," Lillian said, finally able to pry her hands away from Mason.

"Wait," he said, "I'll take you."

Lucy's eyes widened, and Lillian thought she was going to have to step in to prevent a fight.

Lucy wasn't looking at Mason, though, and Lillian quickly saw the focus of her gaze.

"Dustin!" A smile spread across Lucy's face and she opened her arms for a hug. "You made it!"

"Hey! Sorry, I didn't mean to interrupt anything." His eyes flicked from Mason to Lillian.

Lillian stared at him, her heart a helpless puddle in her chest. "Is everything okay?"

He hesitated, then said, "I wanted to talk to you. There's something you deserve to know."

Mason, not one to be ignored, interrupted him. "I'm talking to Lillian right now."

Dustin turned and narrowed his eyes, taking a step toward him. He was half a head taller than Mason, and the difference was stark.

"Are you?"

Mason straightened his shoulders and leaned in. "Why are you always hanging around my girlfriend, man? Don't you have some bunnies to film?"

Dustin stepped away before turning his gaze on Lillian. "You can't be serious about this guy."

She opened her mouth, but nothing came out. Was he... jealous? Angry? What did he care if she got back with Mason? Not that she wanted to, but still.

"Excuse me?" Mason stopped. His lips curled, then, his brow furrowed. "What is this? Are you two..."

"Not the brightest bulb in the tulip field," Lucy muttered, shaking her head and hooking her arm into Mason's. "How about we get you a cupcake?"

"No thank you," he said, tugging his arm away. "Lillian, I need to talk to you. In private."

"There's an idea. Why don't you tell her about Joey?" Dustin said.

"Why don't you mind your own business?" Mason snapped, his right hand balling into a fist at his side.

Lillian stepped between them. "I don't know what is going on, but both of you need to calm down."

Lucy flashed a smile. "Good idea. Let's take this outside." She walked to a nearby door and popped it open. "After you, gentlemen."

Amazingly, they both walked through, and Lillian got a second to whisper to Lucy on their way out. "What is going on, Lucy?"

"I think they're about to fight over you." She let out a dreamy sigh. "I wish Rob would fight someone for me."

"Lucy!" Lillian's voice was hushed, but firm. "That's not funny!"

She shrugged, grinning, and escaped outside. Lillian had no choice but to follow.

Dustin and Mason were already bellowing at one another, their voices carrying across the outdoor patio.

"You need to mind your own business," Mason said, his lips colorless and tight.

"Tell her." Dustin nodded toward Lillian. "Tell her about Kara."

"Get out of here!"

This was ridiculous. They weren't fighting over her. They were just fighting and making a good run at ruining her mom's day.

"Enough." Lillian stepped between them. She had no qualms about yelling over them now that they were outside. "Stop it! What is the matter with the two of you?"

"There's nothing wrong with me," Mason insisted. "He's causing trouble. Tell him to leave, Lillian."

She rolled her eyes. "Okay, Mason."

"What, don't you want him to go? Is he your new island fling?"

If only he knew. "No. He's my...friend." She stumbled over the word, unable to look at Dustin for more than a second.

He seemed to have no problem looking at her, though. His eyes were calm, his voice softened. "Did he ever tell you about Joey?"

Lillian stared at the ground, searching her mind. "I don't know a Joey."

Mason rushed to speak. "He's just trying to get between us. Ignore him."

"Stop trying to boss me around," she said impatiently. She was going to add "There is no 'us'," but Dustin spoke again.

"He's right. I am trying to get between you." Dustin let out a breath. "But only because you deserve to know, Lillian."

"Deserve to know what?" She looked at Mason, her eyes full of questions, but he offered nothing.

"Joey is Mason's son," Dustin said. "The son he abandoned."

Lucy let out a laugh, but Lillian had no reaction. She stared at Dustin, his face serious and creased.

Mason didn't have a son. Surely she'd have known if he had a son.

She looked at him, expecting him to deny, or argue, or dismiss it, but he was silent.

Lillian blinked. "What?"

"I was going to tell you, Lil. After we got married," he finally said.

She gaped at him. "Is this a joke?"

He shot a hurried glance at Dustin. "He's just trying to make me look bad."

Dustin scoffed. "You make yourself look bad."

"Shut up!" Mason put his hands on her shoulders, pulling her in. "Listen to me, Lil, it's not like that. His mom wants nothing to do with me, but I've still been paying child support all these years."

Her mind spun around the words. "*Child support*?"

"Obviously when we got married, I would tell you. It'd be part of the prenup, because then it'd be your money too, but –"

"How is it always about money with you?" She broke free from him. "You have a *son* you never told me about? How can you –"

"It's not that simple." He let out a sigh. "It was so hard for me. You don't understand."

"Well!" Lucy let out a whistle. "I think I'm going to go back inside."

"Hard for *you*?" Lillian put her hands up. "I can't listen to this. I'm going with you, Lucy."

She was halfway inside when Mason called out. "Wait! You don't know everything about Dustin, either. He's been hiding things from you."

Lillian paused. She turned to look at them both, standing there with the ocean at their backs. All she wanted to do was run – cut across the ballroom, through the lobby and get away, away, away.

But that wouldn't solve anything. She couldn't keep avoiding her problems, and she couldn't keep hoping Mason would take the hint and let her go.

She took a step back outside and shut the door behind her. "Go home, Mason. It's over."

Chapter Twenty-five

Dustin stood, hands in his pockets, watching it unfold.

"What are you smiling at?" Mason asked, eyes wild. "Why don't you tell her about what you and Gunther are really doing here?"

Dustin raised an eyebrow. "Trying to film some whales? You're right, you've discovered our diabolical plan."

"That's just your cover."

"You need to go home," Lillian said firmly. "I don't want to see you again. It's over, Mason. It's been over. I'm done."

Mason pointed a finger at Dustin. "This whole show is an excuse to schmooze the guys over at the Bureau of Ocean Energy Management."

"Never heard of it," Dustin said.

"I bet you're going to say you've never heard of offshore drilling or seismic airguns either?"

Dustin shrugged. He'd heard of offshore drilling, but his show had nothing to do with drilling. It certainly wasn't part of Gunther's brand.

"You're helping them get oil drilling rights around the islands."

How absurd. A half smile on his face, Dustin looked at Lillian, fully expecting her to return his amusement. Instead, she was staring at Mason, though her eyes seemed focused far in the distance.

She couldn't possibly believe him, could she? Why was she willing to give him so many chances?

"Is that the BOEM?" Lillian asked slowly.

"Yeah." Mason nodded. "Lil, I can explain what happened with Joey. It's not a big deal, and it's all in the past. If you let that get between us, you're throwing away seven years together."

She flinched, and in an instant she focused her gaze on him. "How can you blame *me* for any of this? You're delusional."

Dustin had to stop himself from breaking into a full grin. She was seeing through him after all.

"Lil, don't be like that." Mason let out a sigh, his voice softening into almost a whine. "I told you how much I've been thinking about what you said."

"You're really good at thinking, Mason. You're always thinking about things, then you turn around and do whatever you wanted to do in the first place." She shook her head. "I'm done with this. It's over. *We* are over. Goodbye."

She shot a look at Dustin before disappearing into the hotel.

Finally. She'd kicked Mason to the curb where he belonged. Dustin let out a breath and the tension left his shoulders.

A few people were watching them. Some of the little audience they'd earned was scattered across the outdoor tables, while others slowed their walks to gawk.

They were waiting for a fight, but Dustin wasn't going to turn his back on Mason, who seemed to be working out the same calculus.

Mason spoke first. "I'm leaving." He pointed a finger. "Stay away from her."

Dustin couldn't help himself. He replied with a simple, "No."

Mason took a few steps toward him and Dustin widened his stance.

Mason stopped, let out a disgusted sigh, then walked off.

Lillian was right. He was all bluster, no action.

Peace returned to the hotel's patio, and patrons resumed their meals and chitchat. Some were surely disappointed the argument hadn't escalated into a fistfight, but Dustin was not one of them. He'd never been in a fight, and he hoped to keep it that way.

He took a seat at one of the tables overlooking the ocean. The water was calm, as always. He hadn't seen a storm or even a windy day make it choppy. This place really was a paradise.

Yet, despite being in paradise, he felt unsettled. At first he thought it was adrenaline from thinking Mason might attack him, but it was more than that. An unease fluttered in his stomach every time he thought of Lillian.

Why had she run off like that? Surely she had to be angry at Mason, not him. Right?

He shifted in his seat. She could possibly be angry with him. He'd just dropped a bomb on her about Mason's son in the middle of her mom's party.

Dustin cringed, rubbing his face in his hands. He hadn't meant to do it like that. It was supposed to be a quiet conversation between the two of them, but when he'd seen Mason with his hands all over her, something snapped.

That was Dustin's problem. He didn't think. He just acted. It was part of what made his history as a hopeless romantic so tragic.

No, *hopeless* was too generous a word. He was a *pathetic* romantic. He could claim he'd only told her about Mason because he was worried about her, and while that was true, there was more to it.

It was all because of her. Lillian. Somehow, she was still the one. After all these years, a glance from her was enough for him to lose his senses. Her laugh was like a siren's call, pulling him to rough waters that would capsize his life.

It wasn't enough that she'd broken his heart, or even that he went on to keep having his heart broken again and again. He couldn't stay away. It was almost as though he hadn't learned anything in the last ten years.

Dustin crossed his arms and took a breath. His head was swimming. It felt like he couldn't hold onto a thought for more than a few seconds.

Was he imagining it, or did it seem like Lillian might still have feelings for him? It was impossible to tell. One minute he could convince himself she felt something for him, and the next he thought she was just being friendly. It was torture, and it made him feel like he was losing it.

Maybe he was. Maybe that was why he told her about Mason's son the way he had. It wasn't the best way to do it, but he meant well.

He could apologize. He could try to find the courage to tell her how he felt, and maybe she would take pity on him and let him down easy this time...

A sharp pain radiated from the back of his head and he lifted a hand to rub the spot. Just another tension headache. Too much thinking and not enough sleeping.

He lifted his eyes for a moment and spotted Lillian. She'd just emerged from the hotel, squinting into the sun, the rays lighting up her face. She was wearing a long, pink dress dotted with tiny flowers. He hadn't noticed it before when Mason kept blocking her with his big, dumb body.

It was like she'd walked out of his thoughts. Dustin's heart leapt and he waved her over.

She smiled before taking a seat next to him and crossing her legs.

"So," she said.

She looked so pretty in that dress.

He sent her a cautious smile. "So."

"Was Mason telling the truth?"

"About Joey?" Dustin shook his head. "No. His mom reached out to me because Joey watches my show, apparently. I can show you the message, but Mason never responded to the poor kid. I got tagged on Mason's Instagram and –"

She shook her head. "I meant about you and Gunther."

He stared at her for a moment, unable to process what she was asking.

"And the offshore drilling."

"Oh." He sat back. "Of course not."

She frowned, looking at her hands. "I saw a card from BOEM in Gunther's room, and something about seismic airguns, too. I know there was."

Ha. He'd hoped she was going to run into his arms and confess her undying love, but instead she wanted to talk about Mason's accusations.

The hope that had buoyed in his chest now sunk deep into his gut, morphing into a heavy mass of shame.

"I don't know anything about it."

Lillian took a deep breath, looking out onto the water, then back at him. "Do you think Gunther might be, I don't know, being dishonest?"

"You mean tricking me?" he suggested.

"Not tricking, exactly," she rushed to say, "but just, I don't know. Something isn't right."

He let out a sigh. "It seems like you believe Mason over me."

"No, that's not it!" Lillian bit her lip. "I'm just worried. What if Gunther is using you, or using the show to –"

"Using me?"

So that was what she thought of him. Dustin let out a scoff, heat rising in his chest. He didn't *want* to react, he didn't want to get upset, but his own shame and embarrassment forced the words out, like a purge, as though they'd be a tonic to his frayed nerves and bruised heart. "Like a pawn? In a game I'm too stupid to see?"

He got up from his chair, suddenly feeling the urgency of needing to get back to work.

"Dustin, no." She stood, stepping closer to him. "I don't think you're stupid."

He clenched his jaw. Of course she thought he was stupid. She probably thought he couldn't land this job for any other reason than the fact that Gunther was using him. "Okay, thanks for that. I have to go."

"Wait." She turned, the sun hitting her eyes at just the right angle – it looked like they were filling with tears. She blinked and the illusion passed. "If anyone's stupid, it's me."

He stared at her, the pained look on her face jarring him back into the moment.

"I need to tell you something." Lillian had her hands together, tight and twisting. "Did you know I never got into Ohio State?"

He opened his mouth to respond, but nothing came out.

"I almost didn't get into any schools," she said. "The only place I got in was into University of Washington. I was wait-listed at the branch campus."

It took him a moment to understand what she was talking about. "What? Why didn't you tell me?"

"It was your dream to go to Ohio State, and I knew I was going to hold you back. That's why I couldn't be with you, Dustin. You were too smart for me, you had too much promise and –" She took a deep breath, her voice catching in her throat. "Maybe I don't always get it right, but I've always wanted..." Her voice trailed off, her eyes now filled with tears. She cleared her throat and stood up. "I've always wanted the best for you. I'm sorry."

Before he could form a semblance of a response, she took off, disappearing down the trail that ran along the water.

The anger and indignation disappeared as quickly as they had flared, leaving him hollow.

School. She'd broken up with him because of stupid school? That was it, all this time?

His phone rang and he silenced it, drifting back into his seat.

He hadn't known about the colleges. It never even occurred to him that Lillian could have broken up with him for something so unimportant.

His phone rang again and, temper rising, he answered. "Yeah?"

Ariel's voice carried through. "We're ready for you, Dustin. Where are you?"

Oh, right. The show he was supposed to be doing. The job Lillian was probably right about. The show he'd been mean to her about, because he was an insecure fool.

He needed to find her, apologize, tell her how sorry he was.

"Dustin!" Ariel said.

"I'm sorry," he said. There was no use chasing Lillian. He'd done enough. He'd made her *cry*.

The sick feeling returned. He was the scum of the earth. The least he could do was leave and give her a break from his neurosis.

He got up from his seat. "I'm on my way."

Chapter Twenty-six

It took walking the hotel's seaside trail twice for Lillian to compose herself. She wanted to pull her thoughts away from Mason and Dustin and focus on something else – anything else.

The harder she tried, the more impossible it became. Her mind was chaos. She felt an urgency to return to the party, and to stop being so self-involved and dramatic. Yet every time she got close to the hotel, panic overcame her and tears welled in her eyes.

Lillian sat on a wooden bench and focused her gaze on the mountain on the other side of the sound.

What had happened? It felt like a jumble, but as she calmed, she could separate the day into two distinct issues.

First, she'd found out Mason was a father – a heartless, absent father. Somehow, despite being with him for seven years, she hadn't known.

Seven *years* with that monster!

Second, she'd found out Dustin hated her. Really, truly hated her, and he thought she was entirely off-base with her suspicions about Gunther. Not only that, he'd taken her accusations personally.

And why shouldn't he?

How had she been so sure Gunther was conning him? Dustin wasn't stupid; she knew that. He was a lot smarter than she was, but in her desperation to get closer to him, she had gone on with her silly suspicions and denigrated the entire production.

It was a disaster. No, she was a disaster, but enough was enough. This day wasn't about her. It was about her mom and Chip – their life, their happiness.

Lillian gave herself ten minutes to soak in her shame, then got up and returned to the party.

When she snuck back into the ballroom, the festivities were in full swing. The string quartet was playing a beautiful rendition of "Livin' La Vida Loca," and a few couples had taken to the dance floor, spinning wildly and bursting with laughter.

Lillian spotted her mom and Chip arm in arm at the dessert table, surrounded by a small crowd. Lucy was at the edge of the dance floor, trying to drag Rob out with her, and presents toppled off the gift table. Beneath, the white table-cloth was sprinkled with glitter, and Margie was busy rearranging the beautiful mess.

At least no one had missed her. That made her feel slightly better. She zigged and zagged her way to the bar, ordering a diet Sprite for herself. Once in hand, she spun around and almost walked into her twin sister.

"Rose!" She put the drink down and threw her arms out for a hug. "You made it!"

"I did!" Rose held her close, rocking back and forth before pulling away. "This party is insane."

"It is. Margie doesn't mess around. I think Mom and Chip are having fun, though."

Rose pulled away and paused, studying Lillian's face. "What's wrong?"

She replied instantly. "Nothing."

Rose lifted her eyebrows. "Don't lie to me. It's written all over your face. And your voice sounds sad. What happened?"

"Nothing," she reiterated, her voice going up an octave.

Rose took her by the arm and pulled her aside. "Is it the arrest?"

She shook her head and peeked over Rose's shoulder. No sign of Dustin or Mason.

That was probably for the best.

"Did they drop the charges?" Rose asked.

"No."

"Oh." She frowned. "You aren't worried about it?"

"It feels like the least of my problems."

Rose stared at her for a moment before speaking again. "You know, you don't always have to be the strong one."

All her sister had to do was take one look at her, and she knew. Lillian took a breath, fully intending to respond, but instead her voice caught in her throat and tears rushed to her eyes.

"It's okay." Rose frowned and pulled her into another hug. "Let's find somewhere to talk."

Rose took Lillian by the hand, out of the ballroom, through the hotel lobby, and into Chip's office.

It was so still compared to the ballroom. Chip's desk was covered with stacks of papers frozen in haphazardly balanced piles. Their mom's desk was much neater, with only her laptop and a few books. Her screensaver was a picture of all of them, the glow from the computer screen bringing a calming stillness to the room.

Lillian took a seat at her mom's desk, and Rose pulled Chip's chair next to her. Then began the storytelling, everything from the moment Dustin had arrived, including her foolish hope that Dustin might still have feelings for her.

"I know it's stupid," Lillian added, "but no matter what I tried, I couldn't stop thinking about him."

"You don't have to explain yourself to me." Rose let out a laugh. "Honestly, I was hoping you and Dustin *would* get back together. It would be one point for true love, and it might mean there was still hope for me and Greg."

Greg. Oy. He was Rose's boyfriend from college, and though they'd been broken up for years, Rose had struggled to get over him.

Lillian knew her sister was sentimental. The last thing she wanted to do was inspire her to keep trying to win Greg back.

"Greg and Dustin have one thing in common," Lillian finally said.

"What?"

"They belong in the past."

They both laughed, and a knock carried through the door.

"It's open!"

Chief Hank popped his head in. "Sorry. I don't mean to interrupt, but Margie said she saw you guys sneak off here."

"Hey Chief. Come on in," Lillian said. It was odd seeing him out of his sheriff's uniform. Regular clothes looked like a costume on him. "Is everything okay?"

He nodded, pulling up a chair. "I don't have the best news for you."

As if this day could get any worse. At least Rose was here now. "Lay it on me."

"Gunther added a charge of theft to the trespass."

Lillian let out a sigh. "Terrific."

"What does that mean?" asked Rose.

Hands clasped in front of him, Hank leaned forward. "It means we're now looking at a felony charge."

Her heart dropped and she sat back in her seat.

"Your arraignment is set for Tuesday," he added. "I'll be there, and I've got a great attorney lined up for you."

Lillian peered up at him. "I need an attorney?"

"Of course you need an attorney!" Rose said, voice high. "How have you not gotten one already?"

Lillian didn't want to admit she had hoped it would all go away on its own. She shrugged.

Hank got up, patted her on the shoulder, and went to the door. "Keep your chin up. I'll have the lawyer call you."

"Thanks."

After he left, Rose turned to her. "All right, listen up. On Tuesday, we're all going to go to the courthouse with you."

"You are?"

She nodded. "You're going to plead not guilty, and then we'll let this Gunther try to prove you're a thief."

Lillian closed her eyes. She could see East Sound in her mind, the mountain in the background, the birds gliding above the sea as their calls carried across the water. She could imagine the sun on her skin, the wind whistling in her ears.

She opened her eyes. "Right."

"I'm not going to let you go to jail." Rose got up from her chair. "We're going to figure this out. I'm going to get Lucy. Maybe Marty, too. Don't worry, okay?"

For the first time that day, her mind was calm. She smiled. "Okay."

Chapter Twenty-seven

He boarded the boat to San Juan Island, unnoticed by the rest of the crew. Ariel had hired the ship, mistakenly booking them to depart mid-afternoon. Gunther had wanted an early morning excursion, and to express his displeasure, he'd decided to shut himself in the bridge with the captain and not speak to anyone.

Dustin didn't have the energy to address it. They were finally going to film some foxes, and he needed to finish memorizing his lines.

It was the perfect time of year to spot the baby foxes, called kits, as they emerged from their dens. He hoped the sight of the fuzzy butts and fluffy tails would lift everyone's mood.

He sat on a bench near the bow of the ship, trying to focus on his script. It seemed too formal. He pulled out a pen and scribbled down an idea. "Feeding the foxes puts them at risk of being hit by cars, so don't do it! And no matter how cute you think they are, don't be fooled – they make terrible pets."

That didn't sound right. He read it aloud, muttering to himself, and scratched out the "don't be fooled." Dustin chewed on the end of his pen, unable to come up with any other phrasing. He stood, looking across the water and onto the islands around them.

"Maybe I don't always get it right..." Lillian had said.

His chest grew heavy and he closed his eyes. All these years, he'd been wrong about her. He'd been wrong about everything. When she'd refused him, all he could see was his own broken heart. He'd never thought about her, how she felt, or the real reason she'd turned him down.

Of course he'd wondered why she'd told him no, and why she'd refused to even discuss it. He assumed, selfishly, that she hated him. Or that his brother was right about her thinking he was too dumb, or too poor, or too *whatever* negative idea his brother had decided to float that week.

It was more likely that his brother had hit on Lillian and gotten shut down. That would explain why he was always so bitterly against her.

Ugh. What a fool he'd been. And still was.

Dustin opened his eyes, focusing on the paper in front of him. *Foxes pounce on their prey like...*

Like what? Like pouncing foxes?

Fixing the script wasn't happening. He was too distracted. He shoved it into his jacket and pulled the zipper to his neck. The boat was moving at a brisk pace, and the wind made it chilly on the deck.

He stood, unable and unwilling to stop the flood of memories. After he and Lillian had broken up, he'd had the brilliant idea to try to make her jealous. He got a new girlfriend as soon as he got to school, and when that didn't get her attention, he'd gotten a different one.

Nothing worked. She never reached out. It was like they'd never known each other. Finally, after nearly a year, he gave up. In that time, she'd met that moron Mason and the rest was history.

Never did it occur to him to *talk* to her. That would be far too mature for eighteen-year-old Dustin. He was too self-absorbed, too self-conscious, and too wrapped up in the drama of his own broken heart to figure out what was going on with her.

To think, it was all because she hadn't gotten into Ohio State! She had been so ashamed that she couldn't even tell him. How pointless it all was.

Of course he would have followed her to the University of Washington. He would have followed her to Fiji if that meant staying together. It wouldn't have held him back. How could she think that? She could never have held him back; she only made him better. One way or another, he would've become a vet.

Or maybe he wouldn't have. Who cared!

He was still a dunce, though – obviously. His neck burned red with shame when he thought of how he'd behaved. It was enough to make him want to sail away and never look back. Maybe in another ten years he could try again.

That would be a coward's move, though, especially since Gunther, who never let go of a grudge, was dead set on sending Lillian to jail over a gift basket.

Dustin didn't know how he would face her again, but the least he could do was make Gunther get over himself and drop the charges.

He made up his mind to confront him on the trip back and get rid of the issue once and for all.

Shooting on San Juan Island went much better than expected. They camped out near South Beach and dozens of adorable kits emerged from their dens to frolic and play for the cameras.

Most of the kits had red fur, only exposing their fluffy white bellies when they rolled over and played. A few were entirely black, save for their white-tipped tails, and every bit as adorable as their red brothers and sisters.

The babies were even cuter than he'd imagined, romping in the tall grasses, thumping their back legs to scratch at their pointed ears, and yawning heartily with their long, pink tongues.

As an added bonus, they got footage of several bald eagles as well, and after a few false starts, Dustin managed to get through all of his fox facts, including the one about not keeping them as pets. While they did look irresistibly soft, one scene of their high-pitched shrieking was sure to convince the audience to stick with cats and dogs.

They returned to the ship once the sun started its descent. The captain offered to take them around San Juan Island to get a view of the sunset, and Gunther cheerfully agreed.

He was back on speaking terms with everyone, and Dustin decided to make his move. He waited until they'd cleared the dock and Gunther had a kombucha tea in hand before cornering him on the deck.

"Looks like we're hitting our stride," Dustin said, sliding onto the bench next to Gunther.

He let out a sigh. "Finally."

"I think we can focus on looking for whales the rest of the week."

Gunther took a swig of his tea. "I'll be sorry if I miss out after all this struggle."

"Why would you miss it?"

He shot a quick glance at Dustin and waved a hand. "I have a thing on Tuesday. On San Juan Island."

"What thing?"

Gunther shook his head, squinting into the red-orange sunlight pouring onto the deck. "Don't worry about it."

He frowned. "Does it have to do with Lillian?"

"I said don't worry about it." He stood up, stretching his arms and letting out a groan.

Dustin wasn't going to let him get away that easily. He stood, following him to the railing overlooking the sea. "You need to drop the charges, Gunther. She doesn't deserve to be in trouble just because you and Ariel had a –"

"This has nothing to do with Ariel," Gunther snapped. "Listen, Dustin, I know you have a thing for her, but we can't just let her get away with what she did."

"What she did?" Dustin let out a laugh. "Dude, she made you a gift basket. It's not exactly the Lindbergh kidnapping."

"No, it's a lot more than that." Gunther turned, squaring off with him. "She's threatening the success of the entire show."

Dustin let out a sigh. "Come *on*."

Gunther dropped his voice. "If we don't stop her, she could ruin everything. I won't have the money to pay you or anybody on the crew. It'll be a scandal."

The wind stung his eyes and Dustin blinked, trying to clear his sight. "She's not going to ruin anything. She was just –"

"I said let it go!"

Ariel skirted by, shooting a smile at them both. They stood silently until she passed out of earshot.

"You know," Dustin leaned in, "Mason came by with a crazy theory about Aaron and this show."

Gunther stared out onto the water, his hands tightening the cap on his bottle of tea.

Dustin started again. "I'm starting to think it wasn't so crazy."

"I'm telling you. You don't want to deal with this. You start tugging at the strings and everything is going to unravel. We need to keep Aaron happy, that's all. Okay?"

"No, it's not okay. What does Aaron have to do with it?" Dustin stared at him, searching Gunther's eyes and finding nothing. "Tell me you didn't make a deal with the devil here, Gunther."

"He's not the devil. He's the one paying your salary." Gunther turned to leave, and when Dustin moved to follow, he threw his hands up. "Stop messing around and get ready to shoot this stupid sunset."

He walked off, and Ariel immediately swooped in to talk to Dustin.

"I need a second," he said, rounding the corner and taking the stairs down to the ship's head.

He shut the door and sat on the small closed toilet. The flimsy door barely muffled the sounds of voices yelling above.

Had Mason been telling the truth? It seemed impossible. Yet the evidence was practically smacking him in the face. Gunther was behaving like a cornered dog.

Was Gunther really going to partner with some oil baron to get this show made? Was he going to help them drill near the islands? How could that possibly be worth it?

It was madness! If a spill happened out here, it would kill everything. The reefs would wilt. The crabs and mussels and salmon would die off. The whales would be scared off by the sound of the guns, and they'd starve to death. There would be nothing to film then but their bloated bodies washing ashore.

If Aaron succeeded, this show would be a documentary of the last days of life on the islands, and to top it all off, Lillian would be the one paying the price.

Why was he insistent on sending her to jail, though? To silence her? To cover it up?

He didn't know, but it was sick. All of it was sick.

Dustin buried his face in his hands. There was no way around it. Gunther couldn't be reasoned with. He couldn't be convinced.

"Dustin!" Ariel pounded on the door. "We've got literal *minutes* to get this shot. Why is it like herding cats to get anything done around here?"

"One second," he called out.

He had a choice. Either he could keep his head buried in the sand and go along with Gunther's scheme, or he could put a stop to it – to the show, to Lillian going to jail, to everything.

It wasn't a choice, really. He didn't even need to think on it.

Dustin opened the door with a smile. "Sorry, still don't have my sea legs. Now what am I supposed to say?"

Chapter Twenty-eight

The lawyer called on Monday and reassured Lillian that he knew the judge, and if all went well, she might only have to spend a few months in jail.

Just a few months.

On Tuesday morning, the troops mobilized for the arraignment. Claire had to be convinced not to throw Gunther's suitcases into the sound. Lucy was quieter than usual, wracked with guilt over her role in Lillian's arrest, but still a force to be reckoned with. Marty took off work to tag along, and Rose stayed after the wedding shower to show her support.

Even Aunt Becca delayed her trip home to make the arraignment, telling Lillian, "I've had more than my fair share of run-ins with the law. There's nothing to do but face it."

"I know," Lillian said.

Her eyes twinkled, and she winked. "What's the worst that could happen?"

Lillian was familiar with the worst-case scenario. It had been playing in her head nonstop. "I go to jail and lose my social work license."

Becca made a face. "Not great, but you can survive it."

She thought on this for a moment. "I guess."

"You can. It's a zen way to tame your worries. What's the worst that can happen? Will I survive it?" Becca paused, tucking a strand of hair behind Lillian's ear. "Once you're through that, try to imagine: what's the best thing that can happen?"

There was something she hadn't thought about. She took a breath. "Well. Gunther changes his mind and decides I didn't commit any crimes, and we all live happily ever after." She let out a laugh. It was absurd to even say that out loud.

Becca smiled. "Don't lose hope. It could all work out, one way or another. However it goes, we'll face it."

Chip rounded them up and dropped them off at the ferry terminal early that morning. "Sorry I can't come," he said, his face in a deep frown. "We've got some contractors coming in to work on the restaurant and –"

"Please," Lillian said, waving him off. "It's fine. There will be plenty of court dates, I'm sure."

She stopped short of finishing that thought. He could come to her sentencing, when the judge would give her ten years. According to Chief Hank, Gunther alleged she'd stolen a six-thousand-dollar camera from his room – conveniently valued high enough to qualify her for theft in the first degree, which carried a maximum sentence of ten years.

She hadn't seen a camera in his room, let alone stolen it! She had no reason to steal from him, but at the same time, how could she prove she hadn't taken something when the police caught her red-handed in the room?

It was nice to have so much support. The one person she hadn't heard from, however, was Dustin. As they walked onto the ferry, with Lucy promising to buy everyone snacks from the galley, Lillian checked her phone again.

Still nothing. No text, no call, no email.

He didn't want to talk to her. He hated her. When was she going to get it through her head?

"Okay, quiet down," Lucy commanded once everyone had taken their seats in the booths lining the windows. "I've scoped out the food. It's a little early for it, but they've got clam chowder. They've got Lopez Island ice cream. They've got croissants, coffee, and caramel corn."

"Forget all of that," Marty called out. "Lillian needs something stronger than caramel corn. Maybe some whiskey in her coffee?"

Lillian shook her head. "I'm not showing up to my arraignment smelling like whiskey."

"Fine," he said with a shrug. "We'll save it to celebrate later."

He had a slight smile on his face. Lillian turned to him, puzzled, but he said no more.

"Clam chowder for breakfast sounds like a good idea," Becca said, sliding out of the booth. "I'll help you, Lucy. Claire, you come with us, too."

"One second." She turned to Lillian. "Are you okay, sweetie? I don't want to leave you here worrying."

"I'm fine." She forced a smile. Her stomach felt like it was stuffed with jelly. "I don't think I can take the smell of clam chowder right now."

She winked. "Got it."

"I'll get coffees," Marty said, getting up to follow them.

Lillian and Rose were left there, sitting side by side, looking out the window. The day was still young, and the sky was a bright blue.

How could it be so beautiful on such a terrible day?

The water was choppier than usual, but the ferry was too large to be bothered, slowly cutting through the waves without so much as a sway.

"It is so pretty here," Rose mused, eyes focused on the horizon. "I'm glad I could stay longer."

"Yeah," Lillian said slowly. "How are you not in trouble at work right now?"

She shrugged. "It's fine."

"I thought you didn't have any more time off," Lillian added. "Did they change their policy or something?"

Rose yawned, covering her mouth with her hand. "No."

Odd. Rose hardly had a moment to spare from work, and now she could suddenly take a few unscheduled days off? Something was up.

"What are you not telling me?" Lillian asked, leaning in. "Did you get a new job?"

"No."

Lillian wasn't going to let this go. "You can't keep that kind of exciting news to yourself."

"I don't have exciting news."

"Something is clearly going on."

"Yeah," Rose said, turning to her. "I got fired."

Lillian gasped and darted a hand to cover her open mouth. "When? What happened?"

"Right before I came for Mom's shower." She hung her head, then let out a breath before straightening her posture. "They put me on an improvement plan, remember? Gave me a mentor, the whole nine yards."

"I remember."

"Well, it was all an excuse to fire me."

Lillian's shoulders slumped. "That's awful. Why didn't you tell me?"

She shifted, uncrossing her legs and stretching out. "I didn't want to bother you when you were in crisis."

"I'm not in crisis."

"Uh huh." Rose gave her a sideways glance. "Don't worry about me. It's fine."

"It's not fine," Lillian insisted. "They've been torturing you at that job for years. And to just *fire* you like that! They can't do that!"

"They can, and they did," Rose said. "You're starting to sound like Lucy."

Lillian let out a huff. "I'm starting to feel like Lucy! I'm going to fly out there, see your ex-boss, and give him a piece of my mind. I should've done it years ago."

"You'll get another felony tacked on," Rose warned, a half smile on her face. "Harassment. Threats, vandalism. Sky's the limit."

"Good." Lillian crossed her arms. "They can add it to my tab."

Rose burst into laughter, and Lillian couldn't help but laugh too.

The rest of her support crew returned from the galley. Becca had a large bowl of clam chowder, and after Lillian accepted a cup of coffee from Marty, she excused herself onto the deck.

The wind cut through her hair, whipping it wildly in front of her eyes. She let it go, cradling the coffee in her hands as the heat radiated onto her skin. It was almost too hot to hold, but she didn't want to let go. She wanted to hang on, to cling to the hope that Becca insisted was still hers, that one way or another, things would turn out all right.

At the courthouse, Lillian had to separate from her party to check in with her lawyer. He told her not to worry, and that today was her day to plead not guilty and to have her rights and charges read to her.

"I don't suspect we'll even need to post bail, but if we do, do you have anyone?"

She looked over her shoulder. Her family had filled out an entire row, bickering in hushed tones. Lucy was pointing at Marty to move so she could sit next to Rose.

It felt like her heart would balloon from her chest. "Yeah. I have someone."

"Good. I'll be right back."

A woman Becca's age leaned over and looked at Lillian. "First time?"

Lillian nodded. "You?"

"Nah." She laughed, breaking into a raspy cough. "The judge is a nice lady. Fair."

Lucy appeared at Lillian's side. "What're you in for?"

"Neighbor keeps accusing me of killing her roses," the woman said. "I haven't gone near her roses. She just has a brown thumb."

Lillian smiled. A far less serious charge than her own.

Or was it? If they couldn't prove the theft, what did they have on her?

She was about to ask more about the judge when she spotted Gunther across the room. He was seated in a chair, alone, his long hair tied into a bun at the nape of his neck. His eyes were focused on his phone, typing away.

"What kind of evidence do they have on you?" Lucy had appeared at her side, apparently eavesdropping on their conversation.

"Nothin'!" the woman replied.

Lucy beamed. "Same as my sister!"

Gunther looked up. For a moment, it seemed like he was looking at her, but his focus seemed zoned out.

Lillian slowly turned and peered over her shoulder just as Dustin breezed past. He paused for a moment to smile at her, the sweet smell of his cologne lingering as he walked on to Gunther. He stooped, whispering something in his ear.

"Is that your lawyer?" the woman asked. "I'd like to get *his* number."

Lucy stifled a laugh. "No, he's not a lawyer." She tapped Lillian on the shoulder. "What's he doing here?"

"I don't know," she whispered.

Gunther looked up at Dustin, eyes narrowed, and put his phone in his pocket before standing up.

"Where are they going?" Lucy asked.

"I don't know," Lillian hissed.

"Well come on!" She grabbed Lillian by the arm. "We need to follow them."

Lillian tugged her arm away. "No!" She dropped her voice. "I don't want to get in more trouble."

Lucy took one look at her, said, "Fair," and scuttled down the aisle to the door.

Lillian bit her lip. Somehow her support team had missed the entire scene. They were busy talking to her lawyer. They had missed Gunther with his man bun, they had missed Dustin showing up. Him smiling at her.

Her heart leapt. He had smiled at her.

She stood from her chair and followed Lucy out of the room.

Chapter Twenty-nine

Gunther had gotten one thing right: it didn't take much tugging to unravel it all.

Dustin was able to fake his way through the sunset shot, and once back on Orcas Island, he got to work. He considered messaging Lillian, but he was still too full of shame, and beyond that, he didn't want to get her hopes up in case he didn't find anything.

His initial goal was to figure out what Gunther and Aaron were up to. That was easy once he knew where to look. Aaron's company had applied for leasing rights to drill off Washington's coast. Some of the waters were so near the San Juan Islands that a single oil spill would contaminate the orcas' food supply and destroy their migration paths. It would be a disaster of historical proportions, and the population would likely never recover.

He dug further. The Bureau of Ocean Management was required to evaluate the environmental impact of any proposed drilling sites, and it seemed Gunther had a plan for this too. Ariel had unknowingly confirmed that Dustin was supposed to personally schmooze a BOEM scientist the following week.

That was easy to put an end to. He sent an email to the guy. "It seems my boss is trying to manipulate you into approving drilling rights for his benefactor, Aaron Forest of Stardust Oil.

I expect you are against bribery and therefore will be agreeable to canceling your visit to Orcas Island, as well as your plans to film the show with us."

The scientist had written back within an hour, saying he was "horrified," and that he would pass the information up the chain. Whether the employee was actually mortified or just embarrassed for being caught didn't matter. The damage was done.

Still, it wasn't enough. As important as it was to prevent the drilling, it did nothing to help Lillian. In fact, it might only make Gunther more spiteful.

Dustin realized he needed help, and after some debate, he reached out to Lillian's cousin Marty. He knew Marty could be trusted, and he was apparently a computer whiz.

The gamble paid off. Marty was able to find things Dustin never could have found. Now all Dustin had to do was play his cards right.

Gunther followed him down the hallway of the courthouse, past the grand framed pictures, past the anxious faces waiting for their moment in front of the judge.

They rounded a corner and found a quiet spot.

Gunther's face was creased with lines. "Is everything okay?"

"No, man. It isn't." Dustin hesitated. This wasn't going to be easy. He wanted to at least give Gunther a chance to do the right thing. "I'm begging you as a friend. Don't do this to Lillian."

He let out a sigh. "Respectfully, Dustin, you have no idea what you're talking about."

"I do, actually. I know what Aaron is planning, and I know why you're part of it. I emailed BOEM. I told them you're trying to bribe one of their employees."

"What?" Gunther's mouth popped open, then he shut it, grinding his teeth for a second before responding. "Why would you do that?"

"We can't be a part of this. We can't let them drill out here. It could kill everything."

"It's not going to kill everything."

"Yes, it will! Do you have any idea what kind of damage –"

Gunther cut him off. "It doesn't *matter*, Dustin. They might do some damage, they might not. Aaron said he might just get the leasing rights so no one can use it to build wind power."

Dustin stared at him. "Are you serious? That's not good either, and even still, he's probably lying to you."

"Whatever. If they drill, they were going to do it anyway. Do you think an email is going to stop them?" He scoffed. "I found out what Aaron was doing and I capitalized on an opportunity. That's business. That's how things work."

As much as he disagreed with that take, it was too big of a life view for Dustin to argue now. "If it doesn't matter, then drop the charges against Lillian."

He shook his head. "It's too late for that. Aaron said he wanted no press around this. We can't have her running off and telling the news about –"

"She's not going to tell anyone." Dustin straightened his shoulders. "But I will."

"Then you're fired." He shrugged, putting his hands in his pockets. "Are we done?"

"What about your brand? Loving the earth and healthy living, all that? Is that just a lie?"

"It's not a lie." Gunther's voice rose, and he paused to compose himself before starting again. "If you try to mess with my brand, I will sue you into the ground."

There it was. The end of niceties, the end of whatever friendship they'd built.

Satisfied he'd won the argument, Gunther spun on his heel and was nearly around the corner when Dustin called out.

"All right, Timothy."

He came to a halt. "What did you call me?"

"Timothy Carrington, of Blueberry Creek fame." Dustin watched the horror round out Gunther's eyes before he went on. "You probably thought no one would ever see your name change announcement in the Benbow Chronicles. It is a small town with, what, no more than four hundred people living there? The website for the newspaper barely works."

"How did you find that?" Gunther rushed in, whispering inches away from Dustin's face.

"I have my sources." He took a step back. "It wouldn't be good for your brand if everyone found out you drained Blueberry Creek and sold off a town's water supply to a water bottling company."

Suddenly Gunther was ready to plead. "Please don't do this. I've started over! I'm a new man. If anyone found out about that..." His lip quivered. "It would ruin my life."

Somehow, Gunther lacked the empathy to see he was doing the same thing to Lillian. Dustin stared him down. "You ran an entire town's wells dry, Gunther. You left them with nothing. They still don't have water three years later."

"I didn't know that would happen!" Tears filled his eyes, hanging at the brims. "We needed the money and –"

Dustin put up a hand. "I don't care. I liked you, Gunther. I thought you were a guy who got things done."

"I am – I mean, I do get things done."

"Yeah. Terrible things."

Gunther looked over his shoulder. "So what, you're going to tell just everyone? Ruin the show, ruin my life?"

Dustin took a deep breath. "I don't have to."

The muscles in his face tightened, then relaxed again. "Is this a threat? If I don't let your girlfriend off the hook, you're going to ruin my company?"

"You mean let her off the hook for a camera she didn't steal and a trespass she didn't commit?" Dustin cracked a half smile. "Yeah, lies like that could really hurt your company."

Before Gunther could say anything else or come up with any more pleas, Dustin patted him on the shoulder and walked away.

Chapter Thirty

Neither Lillian nor Lucy scrambled quickly enough to get out of the way in time, and Dustin walked right into them.

"I'm sorry," he said hurriedly, putting a hand on Lillian's shoulder.

She turned and offered a sheepish smile. "Hi."

"Oh. Hi." He pulled his hand away. "Are you..." He scratched the back of his neck. "Heading in?"

She nodded. "Are you?"

He opened his mouth to respond, but Lucy cut him off. "Want to sit with us?"

"Sure, yeah." He waved a hand. "After you."

Lillian locked eyes with Dustin and her heart leapt.

She needed to say something. Should she acknowledge she'd been eavesdropping? Apologize? Thank him? Ask if he was still angry at her?

He could be angry but still be willing to help her. Yet to blackmail his boss like that...surely the show would be over.

Unable to put these thoughts together, she mumbled, "Better hurry back," before turning away from him and walking into the courtroom.

Inside, it looked like nothing had changed. Lillian's rose-killing friend was still sitting near the front, chatting with a man sitting one row behind her. The judge's chair remained empty, looming tall above them, and Lillian's lawyer was talking to the bailiff and laughing.

Lillian hesitated, unsure where to go, and Lucy gently touched her shoulder, taking the lead. She made her way into the row where their family was camped out. Two strangers had foolishly taken seats there, and Lucy asked – ordered, really – them to move.

"How hard is it to guard two seats?" she hissed at Marty once they sat down.

He shrugged, a grin on his face, and when he caught Lillian's eye, he winked.

What had gotten into him? Lillian cocked her head to the side and lowered her voice. "What's going on?"

"I'm just...hopeful," he said.

She narrowed her eyes, but before she could ask him about this, her lawyer spotted her.

He waved a hand before walking over. "Looks like we'll be tenth to go, but I don't think we're getting any surprises. All I need you to do is enter into a plea of not guilty when the judge asks you. Can you do that?"

Dustin, who had briefly disappeared, reappeared and took a seat next to Lillian.

Her stomach flipped.

"Did you catch that?" her lawyer asked.

She turned, smiling. "Sorry. Yes, not guilty. Got it."

"Great. You can relax until then. When it's your time, we'll go up together."

She nodded, then peered over at Dustin. If he was sitting with her, surely it meant he was on her side?

He leaned in, his forehead almost touching hers. "How are you doing, really?"

He was so close she could kiss him.

Better not. "I'm not bad. How are you?"

"I'm fine," he said, smiling. "I'm not the one on trial, though."

She looked at her hands. He certainly didn't seem angry at her anymore. "I'm good, actually."

A voice boomed, "All rise," as the judge emerged from her chambers.

Lillian stood, bumping her shoulder into Dustin just as she felt a brief squeeze of her hand.

A breath caught in her throat.

The judge took her seat, glasses balanced on the end of her nose, and the bailiff announced, "You may be seated."

Lillian sat, hands clasped in her lap, the warmth returning to her skin.

The proceedings went on for an hour. There was the rose killer, a habitual leash law breaker, a man with an expired registration, a vengeful neighbor who had run over a mailbox, and some teenagers who had been caught drinking in one of the parks.

All allegedly, of course.

When the judge finally called her name, Lillian shot up from her chair, her legs trembling as she made her way to the front.

"Lillian Woodley," the judge said, reading from a stack in front of her. She paused. "Hang on."

She shuffled the papers around and the bailiff stepped forward, handing her a note.

Her eyes scanned it, and when she reached the bottom, she lifted her eyebrows. "It looks like the complaint against you has been dropped."

Cheers erupted from behind her, and Lillian looked over her shoulder to see her support row on their feet.

"All right, relax," the judge said with a laugh. "Case dismissed, and please take your cheerleaders with you."

"Yes, Judge," the lawyer said. "Thank you very much."

He jerked his head toward the door. "You're out, kid. Easiest case I've had all month."

It was like all her limbs had gone numb. She'd forgotten how to breathe, and a small cough choked out of her. Lillian managed to mutter a quick "thank you" before escaping through the back.

Chapter Thirty-one

Outside the monotone walls of the courthouse, the world was bright and alive. A butterfly floated in front of Dustin, inches from his face, its wings yellow and tipped with black stripes.

Was it a Western Tiger Swallowtail? The first he'd seen on the islands or, perhaps, he hadn't been looking closely enough.

It floated away and he followed it up into the endless, rich blue sky. The intensity of the sun was balanced by a cool ocean breeze and at last, it felt like peace had returned to the island.

It all worked out. Though he hadn't been able to appeal to Gunther's humanity, he'd still managed to scare him. He'd take it.

On the sidewalk, Lillian was surrounded by her cheerleaders, as the judge had called them – Claire, Margie, Rose, Becca, Lucy, and Marty.

It felt rude to interrupt and it seemed like, at any moment, they'd lift her onto their shoulders and carry her away.

Before that could happen, an officer emerged from a police cruiser and waved at them.

"Hank!" Claire called out. "They dropped the charges!"

Hank took off his sunglasses and tucked them into his shirt pocket. "I just heard! Sorry I couldn't be there."

"Was it your doing?" Margie asked.

Lucy let out a laugh. "Oh, no, no, no. Chief Hank can't take credit for this one. This was all Dustin."

Suddenly, every face was looking at him.

"I had a word with Gunther." Dustin stepped closer. "He realized how absurd he was being. That was all."

Hank lifted an eyebrow. "A word?"

"A few words," Dustin said with a shrug.

His lips turned down, and he nodded. "Nice work."

Dustin sent a cautious look to Lillian, but she was distracted. Claire had an arm around her and was whispering something in her ear.

"Is it time to celebrate yet?" Marty asked. "I'm starving."

"Yes!" Margie clapped her hands together. "I can throw something together if you want to come back to my house?"

"We're not going to make you host us," Claire said, shaking her head. "We can walk to town and find a table somewhere. My treat."

She looked at Lillian, who put her hands up. "Whatever you guys want to do. I'm just happy to not be in a cell right now."

"We don't have time to celebrate *too* much," Lucy said. "We need to figure out what to do next."

"What to do next?" Rose tilted her head. "About what?"

Marty was already walking down the sidewalk. "Yeah, Lucy. We can discuss over a large serving of fried potatoes."

Lucy went after him, taking long strides. "Fried potatoes?"

"French fries. Tater tots. Hash browns," he yelled. "I'm not picky!"

Rose ran to catch up with them, and Becca took Claire by the arm. Margie gave Hank a kiss on the cheek before following, leaving Dustin and Lillian to trail behind.

It took a minute before they spoke of anything other than the weather.

"I overheard what you said to Gunther," Lillian said, shooting a glance at him. She opened her mouth twice before getting out a "thank you."

He fixed his eyes on the sidewalk ahead. "You're welcome. I'm sorry it took me so long to figure out what was going on. I'm sorry I was a part of it to begin with."

She looked up at him. "I'm sorry you lost your job."

"Some job." He scoffed. "Gunther had no idea what he was doing. I should've known it wasn't going to work when every scene ended up with the crew at each other's throats."

"You can't blame yourself for that. I would've assumed that's just how show business is. I mean, Lucy always had all kinds of problems with show business."

"Lucy? She tried to get into show business?"

Lillian shook her head. "Sorry, bad joke. I meant Lucy from *I Love Lucy*."

A laugh bellowed out of him. "Oh, right. Of course. That Lucy. Why wasn't I thinking of *that* Lucy."

"We all loved that show growing up," Lillian said, a smile dancing on her lips. "It's pretty much all I know about show business, though. Poor Lucy."

He laughed again, turning to look at her. The color had returned to her cheeks, and her lips were no longer a pale pink. "The truth is, I didn't see it because I didn't want to see it. The production was a mess. Gunther was a fake."

"I don't think he knows he's a fake, though."

He smiled. "You're right. He can justify every move he makes. He's one of those guys who is confident all through his failures."

They'd reached a restaurant overlooking the harbor. Lucy had already herded everyone in, but they resisted, instead hanging outside the door.

"You're not the first one to be tricked by an overly confident person."

"You mean like the entire crew who thought I could pull this off?"

She shook her head. "I meant Mason, not you. For so many years I assumed he was right about things because he seemed *so* confident." She let out a sigh. "He could talk circles around me. It was all bluster. You have to know I had no idea about his son."

"I know." He cleared his throat. "I knew he must've lied to you. I thought you deserved to know the truth, especially if you were going to, I mean, if you were thinking of..." He couldn't finish the sentence.

"Yeah." She nodded. "I wasn't, but thanks."

Ah. So she hadn't still been in love with him. It was his own insecurities rearing up, as usual.

That was one thing he could've learned from Mason: unfounded confidence.

The door to the restaurant flung open and Lucy stuck her head out. "Are you coming or not?"

Dustin was tempted to say, "Not." He wanted more time with Lillian.

Maybe if they could stroll along the water and listen to the birds and the blaring of the ships coming into the harbor, maybe he could tell her. Maybe he'd be able to look her in the eyes and finally say what he was really sorry about, how he really felt, what a fool he'd been.

"We're coming," Lillian said, stepping to the door and holding it open. "Dustin?"

They didn't get another chance to talk alone. Lucy led them through the restaurant and out onto a patio, the water shining and sparkling beneath them. Before they were even seated, she started barking orders.

"Okay, Dustin. Tell everyone what you found out about Gunther."

He'd wanted to pull out Lillian's chair for her, but she was already slipping into a seat next to Claire.

He flashed a half smile. "Lucy, were you spying on me back at the courthouse?"

"I can't help that you were blabbing things in the middle of a public building." She pointed a finger at him. "Talk."

He resisted the urge to tease her and did as he was told, starting with the discovery of Gunther's failed skincare line, then going onto the destruction of Blueberry Creek.

"Marty is the reason I even found any of this," he said. "Gunther tried to bury his name change in a tiny newspaper. That was the key, though. It showed who he really is."

"Can't hide anything from me." Marty's voice was muffled, his mouth full of the bread that had been dropped off at the table. "The trick was writing a code to scrape the –"

Lucy interrupted him. "Now Gunther is helping Aaron's company to get rights to drill for oil in the waters around the islands."

"No!" Margie let out a gasp. "How can they do that?"

"There's a process, and it's not easy." Dustin said. "Though it seems like they're well underway. Gunther is convinced it'll happen regardless if he's part of it or not, so he figured it didn't matter if we took Aaron's money for the show."

"That's lazy logic," Lucy snapped. "The old 'if I don't take advantage, someone else will.'"

Dustin agreed, but he didn't think they could do anything about it, so he fell silent.

"If he *really* thought nothing could affect it, he wouldn't have been so forceful about keeping Lillian quiet," Rose said.

"That's a very interesting point," Becca said with a nod.

Lucy drummed her fingers on the table, then pulled out her phone.

"I didn't even put any of this together after going in his room," Lillian said with a sigh. "I saw some things on his desk, and I thought it was odd, but I didn't –"

Lucy's eyes shot up from her phone and she cut her off. "That's why that creep had pictures of me!"

"Not because he's secretly in love with you?" Marty suggested.

Margie and Claire giggled, but Lucy pretended not to hear it. "He knows I've brought down big companies before. He knows I could hurt them. Look at this." She waved her phone at the table.

Lillian reached out to grab her hand. "Okay, no one can see what you're showing us when you move around like that."

"Fine," Lucy dropped the phone. "Listen, drilling leases have been stopped before."

Dustin didn't realize it, but he'd made a face.

Lucy caught it instantly. "What? You don't believe me?"

"No, it's not that. It just seems impossible to go against huge corporations."

"Ha! That's what they *want* you to think! But it can be done."

Dustin leaned forward. "How?"

"Contacting governors. City Councils. Senators. Look at this – Seattle wrote a resolution opposing drilling in 2018."

"And it worked?"

"Yes!" She yelled. "We just need to get moving."

Lillian put her hands on the table and took a breath. "What's next, then?"

"People need to know what's going on. They deserve to know." Lucy bit her lip, staring at her phone. "We need to work fast. It says they're going to announce leasing rights in August."

Dustin slowly moved his eyes toward Lillian. He cared about the drilling – of course he cared – but it seemed all the more important because Lillian cared, too.

He cleared his throat. "So we need to figure out how to alert people. Can't be that hard."

"Do you think you can get your YouTube subscribers to spread the word?"

His mouth popped open. "I hadn't even thought of that."

"Clearly," she said impatiently, pressing on. "Maybe Lillian can help you? Marty, Rose, and I will work on harassing some senators."

Marty frowned. "Hang on. I don't know if I want to harass anyone."

"I mean *contact* them," Lucy said, already typing away on her phone. "Insistently, though. We can't let their staff brush us off."

"Sure, sure," Marty said, letting out a heavy sigh. "Do you think Rob knows anyone who –"

"I'm already messaging him!" Lucy said, shooting a look.

Marty laughed and took a sip of his soda. "Great."

"What about me? What can I do?" asked Claire.

"And me!" Margie added.

Lucy looked up from her phone and without missing a beat said, "Kick Gunther out of the hotel. Margie, you mobilize the good people of San Juan Island. Becca, get some of your hippy friends riled up."

Margie clapped her hands. "I'll contact the paper. One of my friends from book club has a son who's an editor there."

"Okay, we don't have time for a meal," Lucy announced, her head swiveling to spot their waitress. "Let me get the check."

"Nah-ah." Claire shook her head and pointed for Lucy to sit. "We're here to celebrate Lillian. We have time for that."

Lucy stared at her for a beat before giving up. "Fine. Dustin, how fast can you get a video made?"

"Considering I'm now unemployed?" He stared ahead, squinting. He could do it in a day, but if he had Lillian's help, he wouldn't want it to go that fast. "Two, three days?"

She nodded. "That'll do. Lillian, keep on top of him."

Lillian put a hand to her head, saluting. "You've got it, boss. I'll get started after my jailbreak meal."

Dustin laughed, and she smiled at him briefly before focusing her eyes back on the menu.

It felt like his heart had skipped a beat, thudding into his ribs and almost forcing him to cough.

Was she just grateful he'd helped her get out of trouble? Or was there something more behind that smile?

He looked down, pretending to study the menu. It seemed he would have to take a page out of Mason's book and lay his heart out in the open.

Dustin peered up at Lillian. She was laughing at something Rose had said, closing her eyes and leaning her head back.

She was full of joy. Relieved, finally, to not have her future on the line. Who was he to spoil that by dumping his pile of feelings onto her?

He looked back at the menu. Mason had made it look easy. The guy never let up, always insisting she wanted to be with him no matter how many times she told him to buzz off.

Dustin wouldn't do that. He *couldn't* do that. But at the same time, he couldn't let her walk out of his life again without telling her the truth.

He made up his mind. Once this video was done, once they chased Aaron off, he would tell her. Just one time, just so she knew, with no pressure to reunite and no pressure to see him again if she didn't want to.

Just his heart, laid bare, with no expectation of not being crushed again.

Chapter Thirty-two

As soon as lunch was done, Lucy ordered everyone outside. "Okay people, if we hurry, we can catch the ferry. Rob said he'll pick us up on Orcas, and we can head to my place to plan."

Lillian wanted to avoid being stuck at mission control without seeming unsupportive. "Our place?" she asked.

"Yeah, sorry. Our place," Lucy corrected.

Rose cocked her head to the side. "Have you ever thought about getting a bigger apartment?"

"What?" Lucy looked up from her phone. "No, why? We can all fit. It'll be tight, but we can fit."

Initially Lillian thought Lucy had been trying to give her alone time with Dustin when she'd suggested they make the video together, but now it seemed that idea had been entirely forgotten.

Lillian still wanted the alone time, though. "I was thinking we might hang back and shoot some of Dustin's video here."

Rose caught her eye and a smile spread across her face. "Oh yeah, good idea."

"Yeah, whatever!" Lucy was already headed down the side-walk. "Rose, Marty, Claire, Auntie Bec – you're with me."

Lillian got a hug from Rose and her mom, and a wave goodbye from Marty and Becca. They then dutifully went after Lucy, single file, like baby ducks following their mother.

"I hope that's okay with you," Lillian said, turning to face Dustin. "I thought we should try to avoid Gunther and the crew for at least the day."

He lifted his eyebrows. "Definitely. I hadn't even thought of that." He let out a breath. "As usual, I didn't really plan ahead about what threatening Gunther meant."

A very Dustin-like thing to do. She couldn't stop herself from smiling like a fool. "You saved me, Dustin. I'll never forget it."

"Good. Then it was worth it." He looked at his feet for a moment before meeting her eyes again. "Whatever the fallout."

They stood on the sidewalk, staring at each other as a group of hikers pushed them apart. Lillian went to one side, Dustin to the other, and waited for them to pass.

Inconvenient timing, so Lillian looked over her shoulder and spotted a quiet place to talk by the marina.

"Want to sit by the water and think things out?" she asked once the hikers were gone.

A smile spread across his face. "Sure."

They followed a path down and found a picnic table behind a statue of Popeye, the Friday Harbor Seal.

"I have a few ideas," Lillian said. "Let me just pull some things up on my phone."

She had an email from Lucy with resources about offshore drilling. She let out a laugh.

"What?" Dustin asked.

"It's Lucy. She already emailed us."

He shook his head. "I'm not surprised."

Lillian clicked on a few of the links Lucy had sent, then paused. "We don't have to make this video if you don't want to. I don't want to mess up your channel."

He made a face. "The only way to mess it up is to feature Mason and upset Joey."

"Poor kid." She frowned. "Did you write back to Joey's mom yet?"

"I tried, but I don't know what to say. Every time I start an email, I end up calling his dad a scumbag in the first paragraph." He stopped. "Oh – sorry, I don't –"

She put up a hand. "Don't be sorry to me. I know Mason's a scumbag." Lillian shook her head. "Took me long enough, but I know now."

"Happens to the best of us." He paused. "My ex-fiancée was a bit of a scumbag, too."

Lillian winced. "She's right up there with him."

He nodded, his eyes focused on the water over her shoulder.

Of course he was still getting over her – not just her, but the whole situation. No wonder he said he didn't believe in love.

Perhaps he never would.

Lillian's heart fell. She was sorry for how she'd broken his heart all those years ago, and sorry for every heartbreak after. Somehow, despite all of it, he hadn't grown hard and cold to the world. He'd still managed to show Lillian the utmost compassion, saving her at great cost to himself.

She cleared her throat. "We can find a way to make it up to Joey. What if we dedicated the episode to him, then wrote to him and his mom, asking them to watch?"

"That's a great idea. 'This episode brought to you by Joey, who was my first viewer to spot one of these oil scumbags in the wild.'"

She clapped her hands. "That's brilliant! We'll work on the oil scumbag phrasing."

"Sure. We can add 'in his unnatural habitat.'"

From there, the ideas flowed. Dustin put together a short introduction to the islands and its wildlife, and Lillian made talking points about oil drilling.

"How should we phrase this?" she asked, an hour into their planning. "The seismic airguns are used for drilling fire every ten seconds. The sound travels over two thousand miles and can go on for weeks or days without stopping."

"I'll cut the 'without stopping,' part. It's repetitive," Dustin said. "I like the rest, though."

"What can we add to relate it to the islands?"

"I have some ideas," he said, looking at the notes she'd typed out. "I can talk about how it scares off fish and injures the orcas and seals."

"Can it make them go deaf?"

"I think so, but I'll double check," he said.

Within another hour, their script was finalized and they were walking down Front Street with the rest of the tourists.

"Oh shoot, do you need to get a camera?" Lillian asked.

"I'm going to let you in on a little secret," he said, leaning in close to her.

A chill ran down Lillian's back. She tilted her head, shortening the distance between them. "Oh?"

"I film everything for my channel using my phone."

"No!" She pulled away, gaping. "You're kidding."

"I'm not. A phone is all you need."

She managed to keep a straight face, lowering her voice. "You should've told me that before I stole Gunther's camera."

A laugh burst out of him. "Next time."

The ferry had just begun unloading passengers into Friday Harbor, and dozens of people and suitcases crowded the sidewalk.

Dustin nodded his head toward a building behind them. "Want to grab a coffee and take refuge for a minute?"

"I'd love to."

They ran up the stairs and into the little cafe, the door dampening the noise from the street below as it shut behind them.

Dustin got a cappuccino, and Lillian got a lavender black tea latte, topped with whipped cream and nutmeg.

It was indulgent, but she was in an indulgent mood. The man who handed it to her looked like a local – tanned skin, grey hair, and a soft smile. He was a handsome older man, surely a pull for the ladies who were sitting at the nearby table, eyeing him.

She thanked him for the drink and chanced a question. "What's the best way to get to Lime Kiln park if we don't have a car?"

He leaned back on the counter, wiping his hands on his apron. "You could take the bus. Or if you're up for some fun, rent mopeds."

She took a sip of the latte and the whipped cream melted in her mouth. *Amazing.* "Mopeds! That does sound like fun. Also, this is *so* good. Thank you again."

"Any time."

"Another question for you," Dustin said. "What would you think of a company drilling for oil around the island?"

The man let out a huff. "I'd think they'd have to do it over my dead body."

Lillian shot a look at Dustin, then back at the man. "That's why we're here, actually. We just found out a company is trying to bid for a lease nearby."

"We're making a video to get people involved, to stop it," Dustin added.

"I'm a retired environmental scientist," the man said. "You should put in your video that there's a spill almost once a year from these offshore drills. No matter what they tell you, the drilling doesn't bring down the price of oil here, because the executives export it out of the country."

Dustin pulled his phone out of his pocket. "Would you want to be in the video?"

He was already taking his apron off. "I'd be delighted."

Lillian couldn't believe their luck. Lucy would *die* when she heard.

They took a seat at one of the tables and the man, named Ken, worked without a script, providing quick facts and in-depth information about the economic and environmental impacts of offshore drilling.

"Hope it helps," he said as he stood, shaking hands with both of them. "Let me know if there's more I can do."

"Margie Clifton will be organizing something," Lillian said. "Do you know her?"

He laughed. "Of course. I'll give her a call." He waved a hand. "Mention my name and you'll get a discount on those mopeds!"

"Thanks!"

Once outside, Dustin spoke again. "I think we're all set for the video. Hunky Ken can be the spokesperson, and I'll just get some footage of birds and call it a day."

Lillian snorted into her tea. "You liked him, then?"

"Oh yeah, he's just about the coolest guy I've ever met."

"And hunky."

He nodded. "So obviously hunky."

Lillian paused her walk down the stairs, looking over her shoulder. "You're not so bad yourself, you know."

She wasn't brave enough to wait for his response, instead trotting down the stairs and onto the sidewalk.

He followed her and, disappointingly, ignored her comment, talking about filming seals near Cattle Point before going on to Lime Kiln to watch for orcas.

"I don't have much hope," he admitted. "We've missed them all month, but maybe I can cut in footage of whales and make it look like they were there."

Lillian didn't care if they saw the whales. She just wanted to savor her time with him. "I'm feeling lucky."

They mentioned Ken's name at the moped rental place and drove off on the little machines practically for free. It was a rocky start, getting used to the freedom of zipping down the open roads, but the trip to Cattle Point was nothing short of magnificent.

They drove along, catching views of the ocean here and there, plunging back into forests, then emerging into wide, open farmland. When they reached the sea again, they were rewarded with sweeping views of the clear sky meeting the dark blue ocean, the fields on either side of the road swaying with golden grasses.

They pulled into a parking lot for the lighthouse and nearby a mass of seals lounged by the beach. They were highly cooperative with being filmed, lazily rolling in the sun and barking at one another as if on cue.

Dustin and Lillian kept a respectful distance, but even still, the stench of fish wafting from them was unbearable.

"Good thing they're so cute," Lillian said, "because they *stink*."

Dustin laughed. "They're up there on the stinkiest animal list for sure."

With a stunning background of distant mountains and sea, Lillian filmed Dustin talking through the script, which he'd somehow already memorized.

Once they were satisfied with the footage, they hopped back on their mopeds and drove to Lime Kiln Point State Park. There were a good number of tourists there, but after hiking along the rocky shoreline, they managed to find a quiet spot to shoot near the lighthouse.

Dustin stood, looking tiny compared to the iconic light-house, and again went through the talking points.

"We'll cut this together later to make it look cool," he assured her.

As if she had any doubts. Lillian knew he was brilliant. If only she could find a way to tell him that so he would believe her...

Nearby, there were a number of tables and benches, all filled with hikers and hopeful whale watchers, some with binoculars around their necks.

They found an empty table and took a seat.

"How are you doing?" Dustin asked. "Are you tired? You must be exhausted after today."

Lillian shook her head. She'd hardly slept the night before, but being with Dustin energized her. Maybe it wasn't special to him, but to her, it was one of the best days she'd had in...well, since she could remember.

He may not realize it yet, but Lillian knew it was inevitable he'd leave the island soon. This video might be their last chance to hang out. She didn't want to miss a second of it, even if it felt like gravity was winning in pulling her heavy limbs down.

"Are you sure?" He leaned in, and for a second it seemed like he was going to put his hand on top of hers. Instead, it came to rest on the rough wood of the bench. "We can pick this back up tomorrow."

She pulled her hand away, sticking it in her pocket. This was what her sleeplessness had done to her. She was imagining something where there was nothing. "I'm fine, really. I'm still riding the high of getting out of jail."

"Ha, that's right." He flashed a smile. "Would you mind coming over to the shore with me? I want to shoot one more thing."

"Sure."

She followed him as he walked onto black and grey rock jutting over the beach. He stood out so beautifully against the backdrop of the sea, with his broad shoulders and the bright white of his smile, as he turned to look at her.

Why couldn't things have gone differently? Why had she gotten a chance to see him, only to lose him again? Life could be so breathtaking and so devastating in the same moment.

Maybe the exhaustion really was getting to her. She felt loopy, like she might cry, but then he offered her a hand. The warmth of his touch pushed the feeling away, filling her chest and steadying her as they teetered on the edge of the vast sea.

They were far enough away that the other voices were drowned out by the sound of the water, and the backdrop was even more stunning than before.

Even if it wouldn't last, she was here with him now. The thought buoyed her spirits, and she widened her stance as she fit him into the frame.

"Careful not to fall," he said, turning so his back was to the ocean. "I'll make it quick. You don't mind recording again, do you?"

"Not at all." She looked down, making sure she was on stable ground, before hitting record and giving him a thumbs up.

He smiled and nodded. "When I was in high school, I knew two things for sure. One was that I wanted to be a veterinarian, and the second was that I wanted to marry my girlfriend at the time, Lillian Woodley."

Her mouth popped open, but she didn't dare move.

He went on. "Lillian is one of those rare people who improves everything she touches. She has a beautiful smile, and a beautiful soul. Even though I was too young to marry her then, I tried." He laughed. "Quite wisely, she didn't agree to it."

Lillian laughed, too, covering her mouth with one hand.

"I've continued to make a lot of mistakes in my life, and gone on to make a fool of myself dozens, if not hundreds of times but one thing I am still sure of. There is no one quite like you, Lillian. I love you, and I think it's safe to say I always will."

She gasped, dropping the phone to her side. "Dustin."

He took a breath, his eyes wide. "I'm not trying to put any pressure on you, Lillian. I just – I needed you to know."

Tears rushed to her eyes and she ran to him, throwing her arms around his neck. "I love you, too," she whispered.

He hugged her tight, wrapping her with the gentle firmness of his arms.

It couldn't be real. It was too good to be real. She pulled back and stared at him. "Why didn't you say anything before?"

He shrugged, grinning. "I didn't want to be too much like you-know-who."

Astonishing. She touched his cheek. "You could never be like Mason."

"Shh," he said, getting close. "We don't say that name here."

"You're right," she whispered back, their lips only inches apart. "My mistake."

Dustin kissed her, and it felt like her feet would lift off the ground.

"They're coming, they're coming!" a voice called out from the picnic tables.

Lillian broke their kiss, smiling sheepishly at him. "I thought they were yelling about us for a second."

"Me too."

He pulled her closer, and she rested her head on his chest. "You're not going to believe this."

"What?" she asked.

"There's a pod of orcas headed right for us."

Lillian looked past him, seeing the first black fin as it broke the water, followed by a spout of air.

Within moments, the whales were upon them, only twenty feet from shore, their blows carrying across the water.

"I think there's one right there, right beneath us," Lillian said, pointing.

Dustin shook his head. "Where?"

They saw the saddle patch first, ghostly white in the clear water. The little orca flipped, her white belly turned to the sky, and she slapped her tail on the surface.

"Whoa!" Dustin jumped. "I can't believe this."

The orca was small, perhaps ten feet long, and she broke through the surface of the water, taking a breath before pausing, opening her mouth and sticking out her tongue.

A larger whale, maybe her mother, popped her head out of the water, looking right at them before disappearing beneath the surface.

"This is the best day of my life," Lillian whispered.

"What did you say?" Dustin asked, looking down at her.

She beamed up, reaching into her pocket. "We'd better get the camera."

Epilogue

In July, the West Coast Chronicles published an interview with Aaron Forest where he admitted his company's plan to lease drilling sites near the islands. He urged locals to accept the "disruption" as a side effect of progress, adding the deal was "essentially done, and as sure a thing as you get in business."

Rose had the pleasure of being in the room when Lucy read the article. She sat back and watched as voices raised, fingers jabbed, and spit flew through the air.

"He's only doing this because he *knows* we're a threat!" Lucy said, pacing back and forth. "He wants to discourage people from trying to stop him."

"Of course," Rose said, looking up at her from the couch. "We don't have to –"

"It's not going to work, Aaron!" Lucy bellowed, eyes wide and wild. "Dustin's video already has four million views, and it's only going up. People are touched by it. *Touched*!"

"That video is a cinematic masterpiece," Rose said with a sigh. "The editing, the whales, the lighthouse with the sunset in the background –"

"Yeah, it was incredible!" Lucy narrowed her eyes. "If Aaron thinks he can trick us into –"

"He's not going to trick us," Rose said, getting up from the couch. "We're on it."

It was getting harder to steer Lucy's outbursts, especially with Lillian gone half the time. She was too busy frolicking around the island with Dustin to deal with their older sister.

To be fair, Lillian had handled Lucy's last series of outrages when Grindstone Farm and the hotel were in trouble. Rose had been absent for all of it, just as she'd been absent for Lillian's breakup with Mason and Lillian's beautiful reunion with Dustin.

There was guilt. A lot of it. Rose had allowed herself to get so wrapped up in her job that she missed out on time with her family. She had fully dived into her job's toxic culture, telling herself it would change, that it would get better after this event, or after a few months, or after they hired support.

It never changed, and what was the point of all her sacrifice? In the end, they had fired her anyway.

Lucy had gotten her a temporary position at Grindstone Farm. It was a pleasant change of pace, especially because Rose's new coworkers weren't constantly cutting her down. Oddly, they even *complimented* her. Even more bizarrely, it seemed genuine! Rose hadn't been praised at her job in years.

The comfortable laidback environment made the days melt away. August came and went, and following an influx of immense public pressure, the governor signed a resolution opposing any offshore drilling, and a bill was proposed in the state senate to ban the practice entirely.

Aaron's bid for a lease was never approved. He sold off his property on Orcas Island and quietly disappeared.

When they got the news, Lucy threw a party at the farm. People from all the islands came to celebrate.

Rose's favorite part of that evening was seeing Dustin become a bit of a celebrity. No fewer than three women approached to fawn over him, trying to flirtatiously touch his biceps as they flipped their hair.

If it had just been one woman, she would've chalked it up to a fluke. The second woman was easily distracted by Lucy, and when the third woman came swooping in, Rose had to turn around to hide her laughter.

Once she recovered her composure, she set her mind to shooing the lady away, but it ended up being unnecessary. Dustin not so subtly put his arm around Lillian as he thanked her for her support.

"Smooth," Rose said once the coast was clear. "I was ready to tell her to buzz off."

"I was ready to tackle her," Lucy said. "How do you put up with it, Lil?"

"I don't mind," she said with a laugh. "I think it's cute."

Dustin grinned. "I swear this never happens."

"It's not his fault," Lillian added, "He's adorable."

"She's right." Dustin nodded solemnly. "But it's not enough to be adorable. I need to stay humble, too."

They all laughed, then made their way to the makeshift dance floor. Lucy had hired a live band, and the floor was packed with revelers. She pulled Rob out onto the dance floor, and Dustin dragged Lillian out, too.

Rose stood off to the side, looking on. The wind blew and she caught a chill, a shiver running down her back. A strange thought floated into her head that she was like a palm tree – out of place and alone.

Then she felt a tap on her shoulder.

"Got a dance for your future not-so-evil stepfather?" Chip asked, smiling tentatively and holding out a hand.

His excitement was contagious. Rose grinned as she accepted his invitation. "Why not-so-evil?"

He shrugged, leading her an open spot on the dance floor. "That's what Lucy calls me."

"You can't take her seriously," Rose said with a laugh. "None of us do."

"Oh, don't worry," he said, spinning her out. "I learned that a long time ago!"

The wedding was a short two weeks later, and as usual for big events, it seemed like it had been coming for ages before completely sneaking up on all of them.

"I don't see where these supposed clips are," Lucy complained as she studied the back of their mom's dress.

They were in the Sunshine Suite of The Grand Madrona Hotel, where they'd all slept the night prior. The plan had been for everyone to sleep in their own rooms, but they ended up getting cots brought up and staying up far too late into the morning hours laughing.

"There aren't clips," Lillian said, lending a delicate hand to the fabric. "Just tiny pearl buttons."

"*Oh*. Elegant!"

"What're you doing back there?" their mom asked, peeking over her shoulder with a smile on her face.

"I'm trying to understand how this isn't going to fall off you," Lucy said, tapping her chin. "I think I get it."

Rose let out a laugh. "It's pretty secure. Mom, twirl around. Show them."

"I'm not going to twirl! It'll mess up my hair." She shot a hand to the chignon-style bun at the nape of her neck. There were a few pieces curled around her face, but the rest of her hair had been expertly twisted and pinned in place by Aunt Becca.

"Twirl!" Becca demanded, clapping her hands. "That hair isn't going anywhere."

Claire laughed, obliging them, and the satin spun out elegantly, catching the light streaming in from the windows. Though the surplice neckline and open back looked precarious, it did indeed stay in place, swaying elegantly as she moved.

Finding the gown had been a joint effort by Margie and Lucy. They'd had to band together after Claire declared she would wear an old dress she already owned.

After a frantic search, they found the perfect dress: a 1930's inspired ivory gown made entirely of satin, with billowed sleeves and a glamorously draped, plunging back.

"It's so romantic," Lillian said dreamily, flopping onto the couch.

"It's so you, Mom," Rose added.

She studied herself in the mirror for just a moment, then turned away. "It's a very pretty dress."

"It's pretty, and you're pretty in it." Becca stood up, hugging her from behind. "No, you're gorgeous!"

"All right, all right." She gave her a squeeze, scanning the piles of clothes and suitcases scattered on the floor. "I'll try not to trip on my way out."

"No tripping on your big day!" Lucy ordered, mouth hanging open as she applied mascara.

Rose couldn't believe it. Her mom was *actually* getting married. When Rose was in middle school, she had always worried her mom would find some awful partner to boss them around, and he'd be scary with a huge mustache like her best friend's dad. She was convinced if her mom found a boyfriend, she wouldn't have time for them anymore.

As she got older, Rose wished their mom *would* find a guy. She didn't even care if he was a bit weird or had goofy facial hair. She just wanted him to be nice to her, and take her to dinners, go on bike rides, or anything. Rose tried pushing her mom to go on dates, but Claire wouldn't have any of it – she insisted she was perfectly happy.

Then came Chip. He was such a delight. Where had he been all these years? Her mom lit up around him. It was like some quiet part of her had come alive for the first time. She laughed more easily, and she had confidence in her ideas and plans like never before. He was always doing little things for her, too – washing her car, planning romantic getaways, making her favorite foods.

Another pang of regret sunk in Rose's heart. She'd missed all of this. Of course she'd talked to her mom on the phone, but it wasn't the same. Her mom had finally met the love of her life, and Rose was only now getting to know him.

"What's the matter?" Lillian asked, leaning in. She was halfway done with her makeup, her foundation delicately blended and her eyebrows painted in, but the rest of her face looked small and washed out.

"You look like a muppet," Rose said, laughing. "You're all eyebrows."

Lillian looked in the mirror and laughed. "Too dark?"

"No, they'll be fine once you color the rest of your face in."

"Okay, stop!" Lillian laughed, covering her eyebrows with her hand. "Don't change the subject to my muppet eyebrows. Why do you look so sad?"

It was impossible to hide anything from her twin. She dropped her voice. "It's nothing, really. I just feel bad I've missed out on getting to know Chip. I'm happy for Mom, but...you know."

"I get it. I felt the same way." She shrugged. "I guess you just have to stay here."

"I guess I do."

Lillian's mouth popped open. "Do you mean it? Are you going to stay?"

She couldn't stop herself from grinning. "If I can find a real job, yes, I'm going to stay."

Lillian clapped her hands together. "Hey everyone! Rose is moving to the island!"

"What!" Lucy jumped up from the floor where she'd been curling her hair. "Are you serious? We need to get a bigger apartment!"

Her mom crossed the room, looking like an old Hollywood star, a hand to her chest. "No, keep staying with me! It'll be like the old days."

"Uh, no." Lucy shook her head. "She can't move in with newlyweds. Obviously, she wants to live with me and Lillian."

"Guys, guys," Rose said, putting her hands up. "There's no need to fight. There's plenty of me to go around."

They laughed, and her mom pulled her in for a hug. "I'm sorry about your job, sweetheart, but maybe this is a silver lining?"

Rose nodded, being careful not to stain her mom's dress with makeup. "I think so."

There was a knock at the door and, before anyone could answer, Margie burst through. "What are you doing? You have ten minutes before we need to leave for the church!"

"That means five minutes until the first look!" Lucy cooed.

"First look?" Margie shook her head. "No. Claire, that'll be at the church, won't it?"

She smiled. "I thought it would be nice for Chip to see me where we first met. Here, at the hotel."

Margie let out a gasp. "That is so sweet."

"At the bottom of the staircase, under the chandelier," she added.

"Stop!, I'm going to cry my makeup off," Lucy said, fanning at her face.

"Yeah, and Lillian might cry her eyebrows off," Rose said, cracking herself up.

"Har har." Lillian shot her a look. "You look like you don't even have eyebrows, so why don't you work on that?"

Rose turned to the mirror, eyebrow brush in hand. "Good point."

They hurried to finish getting ready.

Their mom wanted the first look to be just between her and Chip, so naturally, as soon as she left, Lucy, Lillian, Rose and Becca ran down the stairs so they could spy from the corner of the lobby.

They got there just in time, huffing and breathless.

"Sh!" Lucy said. "Lillian, why do you breathe like a bull-dog?"

"My nose is stuffed," she hissed.

"Both of you, quiet!" Becca whispered. "She's going to see us and we'll all be in trouble."

Chip, waiting at the bottom of the grand staircase in a navy suit, didn't seem to notice them. Or at least he pretended not to, his eyes fixed above.

They half-walked, half-ran and squatted behind a couch, trying to get a better view of the scene. Rose peeked over the back of the couch just as her mom appeared at the top of the stairs.

She was a vision. Light radiated off her and the elegant dress. There seemed to be a glow around her shining hair.

When her eyes met Chip's, the biggest smile crossed her face. "Hi."

They could only see the side of Chip's face – he, too, had the biggest grin. His shoulders dropped. "You are so beautiful."

"I think he's going to cry," Lucy said in a hoarse whisper.

Becca elbowed her. "*Sh!*"

Chip went up the stairs at the same time as Claire came down, her hand on the golden railing. They met on the landing and he took her face in his hands, whispering something before kissing her on the cheek.

She was beaming, and she took a step back before delicately running a hand from his shoulder to his chest. "So handsome, Mr. Douglas."

They both laughed and he offered her an arm to walk down the stairs.

The four of them ducked behind the couch again, whispering and giggling until a voice boomed above them.

"I see you back there," she said.

Rose looked up, covering her mouth. "Sorry, Mom."

"Sorry, Mom," Lillian and Lucy said in unison.

"Sorry, *Mom*," Becca said, laughing.

"You ladies need a ride?" Chip asked, eyes bright. "Plenty of room in the limo I rented."

"A limo!" Rose clapped her hands together. "Don't mind if I do."

Her mom took a deep breath and smiled. "I'm so happy you're all here. I'm so happy we get to be together."

There were tears in her eyes, and Lucy popped up and put an arm around her. "Don't cry, Ma. We're happy to be together, too."

She started leading her away, followed by Chip and Becca. Lillian and Rose stood and linked arms.

"I'm glad you're here, too," Lillian said, popping her hip and bumping into Rose.

"Thanks. I'm pretty happy myself," Rose said, bumping her back. She sighed. "Let's make sure Lucy doesn't scare away our new stepdad."

Lillian nodded. "Good idea."

The Next Chapter

Introduction to *Sunset Serenade*

After Rose finalizes her move to Orcas Island, a misunderstanding lands her a job as a professional matchmaker. Though she doesn't *technically* have the qualifications they think she has, Rose is sure she can excel in her new chosen career.

That is, until she breaks her own rule and falls in love with the one man who is off limits...her boss.

Get your copy of *Sunset Serenade* today!

Would you like to join my reader group?

Sign up for my reader newsletter and get a free copy of my novella Christmas at Saltwater Cove. You can sign up by visiting: https://bit.ly/XmasSWC

About the Author

Amelia Addler writes always sweet, always swoon-worthy romance stories and believes that everyone deserves their own happily ever after.

Her soulmate is a man who once spent five weeks driving her to work at 4AM after her car broke down (and he didn't complain, not even once). She is lucky enough to be married to that man and they live in Pittsburgh with their little yellow mutt. Visit her website at AmeliaAddler.com or drop her an email at amelia@AmeliaAddler.com.

Also by Amelia...

The Orcas Island Series

Sunset Cove

Sunset Secrets

Sunset Tides

Sunset Weddings

Sunset Serenade

The Westcott Bay Series

Saltwater Cove

Saltwater Studios

Saltwater Secrets

Saltwater Crossing

Saltwater Falls

Saltwater Memories

Saltwater Promises

Christmas at Saltwater Cove

Standalone Novels

The Summer Request

The Billionaire Date Series

Printed in Great Britain
by Amazon